Sirens & Scoundrels

Tales from the Quaquaverse, Volume 2

A.P. John

Published by A.P. John, 2024.

SIRENS & SCOUNDRELS

First edition. June 13, 2024.

Copyright © 2024 A.P. John.

ISBN: 979-8986620459

Written by A.P. John.

Also by A.P. John

Tales from the Quaquaverse
A Horse for My Kingdom
Sirens & Scoundrels

Watch for more at apjohn-author.com.

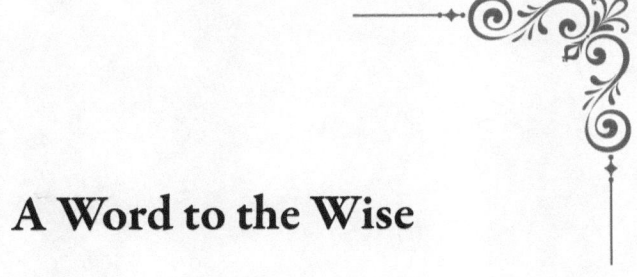

A Word to the Wise

FROM A.P. JOHN

Let the Reader Beware

What follows is not necessarily a good story, well told. But it is a story. That much I guarantee.

I wrote this story because it gave me a laugh and a tingle in my trousers. I put it into your hands to give you the same pleasures. The sense of humor is my own, perhaps only my own, and to that end it is rife with sex, violence, toilet humor, puns, parody, farce and slapstick. The violence and jokes are included primarily to fill the spaces between the sexy parts.

Most important, dear reader, understand this is an *adult fantasy* story, with emphasis on *fantasy*. If you seek laughter and titillation, you're at the right window. If you are looking for anything else, like *A Story of Great Moral Import* or, gods save us, *A Good Example for the Children*, you will find what you seek over there, in that rapidly growing library section overseen by the humorless and perpetually outraged ochlocrats in the Ministry for Ruining Everybody's Fun.

In short: *Ye buys your ticket, an' ye takes yer chances.* **Caveat Lector.**

Chapter 1 - Her Pleasure Cruise, Interrupted

Lady Ravenna Ferdinand, young and lovely and infuriatingly blond, stood on the deck watching the afternoon sun glisten on the calm waters of the Plymouth Sea as the three masted corvette *Bentley* cut deep wake under full sail to carry her homeward, there to marry and happily surrender her virginity.

"I shall miss the convent in Packard" she said wistfully, the ocean breeze hardly mussing her ludicrously long, blond, flaxen locks, "but my heart belongs to my beloved, and I am ready to give it over to him completely."

"Yes, mistress" said the short and wizened Sister Adelaide. She gripped her veil tight around her withered neck against the wind. "Two days hence you will be wed, and you have prepared yourself well."

As shining and flowing as the flag of her tresses, Ravenna's luxurious silk gown of azure blue fluttered in the wind. She pulled the delicate lace shawl tighter about her shoulders. "I'm so happy they allowed you to accompany me, dear Adelaide. Prepared or not, I feel I must have your continued guidance as I approach my wedding day and the inevitable rough-but-loving coitus that awaits me in the marriage bed."

"Well, m'lady, it need not be rough."

The rose hue in the girl's porcelain cheeks betrayed her thoughts. "No? But is it not true, as you and the sisters taught me, that a husband may take his pleasure as he will, ravishing his quarry with impassioned tongue kisses, tearing her bodice open to feast on her heaving breasts,

1

lifting her skirts and bending her over the soft velvet bolster of the chaise lounge to-"

"Ahem" the squat nun interrupted, blushing herself, "yes, all that might indeed be your lot. But then again, the good captain might be inclined to more gentle pursuit of your tender favors."

"Might he? Oh, dear."

Ravenna turned to gaze over the prow toward the western horizon, beyond which lay the Duchy of Hudson. The fast ship would make port there in a few short hours, returning the lady to her home after a year in convent. Her father the Duke Argo and her mother the Duchess Gleda awaited her arrival, making lavish preparations for her wedding to the brave and impeccably groomed Captain Ozymandias Wembleye.

"I do hope not," she whispered.

A deck hand hurried to the women and held out a parchment, carefully folded and sealed with a red wax stamp.

"Beggin' yer pardon m'lady, but this arrived with our cargo 'afore we left port at Packard this mornin.'"

Ravenna took the envelope and ignored the sailor as she read the salutation.

When Adelaide saw the man staring lustfully at the young lady's taut but ample breasts, she reached out and gave his ball sack a quick slap.

He grunted and doubled over, eyeing the old woman with surprise, then scorn.

"Off with you" she growled, "or take my foot to thy yarbles, thou starveling bulls-pizzle."

As the man limped away, Ravenna's eyes blazed with joy.

"It's from my beloved Oz!" she gushed, bouncing on the balls of her feet with excitement. Her thick, irritatingly shiny hair flashed semaphore in the deepening late day sunlight.

She broke the seal and spread open the parchment, scanned the first line and announced, "I must retire to my quarters to read my dear captain's love letter properly. Have all my belongings been stowed aboard this vessel?"

"Yes, dear girl, but only the trunk with your essentials has been placed in your cabin."

"Then go and fetch the Penis Portmanteau immediately and return as quickly as possible. I must prepare!"

"At once, mistress" said the aged sister.

As Adelaide shuffled off toward the cargo hold, Ravenna skipped girlishly to the small room allotted her near the captain's cabin and closed the door behind her. She twirled with delight several times, holding the letter to her breast, then stopped and closed her eyes, her breath shallow and fast.

"Oh my dear, dear Captain Ozymandias" she whispered, "how long we have been apart. But soon we will become one in wedlock and never be separated again."

Thinking back on her year of training at the hands of the Sisters of Saint Salacious, her eyes sparkled, and her grin turned wicked.

"Won't you be surprised" she purred, "when you learn how ready I am to receive your animal lust."

She opened the parchment and began reading aloud.

To My Darling the Lady Ravenna Ferdinand, Song of My Heart.

The girl caught her breath and sighed, then read on.

This morning I enjoyed a particularly splendid bath. The water was a perfect middling temperature, not overly hot but not tepid, and the bubbles ideal in volume and texture so as to form a lovely relief map of peaks and valleys. The scented soap delivered a delicious admixture of lavender and rosemary, sweet and savory, and so naturally my thoughts drifted toward you and the nearness of our upcoming nuptials, now a scant few days off.

Transported as she read, Ravenna's delicate fingers drew a soft line from the hollow in her throat to a point deep within her cleavage. She felt herself stir, a warmth infusing her inner thighs. She read on, now too breathless to speak the words, able only to mime them with pale, trembling lips.

I am told your father and mother have devoted considerable time and resources to the ceremony of our joining...

Ravenna balked and gasped slightly, her mind afire with wanton images associated with the word, *joining.*

...and so we are assured a lavish affair, full of pomp and parade. If you don't deem it impertinent of me, I believe I shall array myself in my finest dress whites with the royal blue piping and gold epaulets and adorn my best fore-and-aft bicorne with the largest ostrich plume I can obtain. Would that please you, my dove?

"Yes" the lady breathed, "yes, my darling man, it would please me to clutch those epaulets while your many glistening medals swing and ring like bells as you hold me down and..."

The door suddenly opened to reveal Adelaide dragging a large case of leather and brass.

"Here, dear lady" she wheezed, "your selections."

Ravenna hurried to lay on the small bed and fought to catch her breath. "Hurry, dear sister, bring it here!"

The aged nun huffed as she struggled to carry the heavy valise. She grunted and set it on a bedside table, undid the latches and raised the lid.

Within, nestled in deep purple velvet, were arrayed seven phalluses carved of various hard materials, each one a reasonable facsimile of that which the Captain Ozymandias Wembleye carried within his breeches.

The first, sculpted of finely grained white oak and polished to a sheen, depicted his manhood at rest, peering down over the double domed encasement of his testicles. The seventh bore the likeness of his fully turgid cock and balls, carved of the finest white marble and given life by the artist's anatomical details of veins on the shaft rising toward the prominently ridged glans.

The remaining artifacts depicted the captain's wedding tackle in the various stages of rest and activity between the two extremes.

It was with such a set of artisanal dildi that the good Sisters of the Saint Salacious Convent trained young brides-to-be to recognize the various stages of male priapic station, what techniques could be employed with each for both her and her husband's pleasure, and to help avoid the typical shock and awe that virginal brides had throughout history been forced to endure during the first attempt at post-ceremony penetration.

Ravenna greedily snatched the seventh from its velvety bed, hiked her skirts to her hips and, legs wide and shaking, plunged it to the hilt into her already bemoistened and quivering quim.

"Ah!" she cried, "Yes, my lusty sea dog! I am helpless against your onslaught of mean-spirited fuckery!"

While one hand impaled herself with the marble manroot, the other lifted the letter to her squinting eyes. Struggling to focus her vision, she continued to read aloud between rhythmic grunts and sighs.

When I think of you my dear Ravenna, and of our impending union in wedded bliss, my heart soars with delight at the thought of sharing not only our conjugal bed...

Ravenna grunted and snarled, "Yes! Harder, you seagoing stallion!"

...but also our conjoined bathing facilities, where I look forward to long and indulgent sessions of lavation together. I picture myself washing and conditioning your lovely tresses...

Panting, Ravenna growled, "Fill your fist with my locks and spur me for the finish line, master of horse!"

...and I hope that you will find my wide knowledge of oils and cremes, scents and conditioning rinses impressive enough to allow me to school you in the finer details of the ablutionary arts.

Head back and eye-rolling in animalistic fervor, Ravenna dropped the letter and two-handed herself into a chest-heaving, spittle-flecking frenzy, no longer possessing the skill of human language or even knowledge of herself beyond the sensations between her navel and her knees.

Watching all this from a safe distance, Adelaide took note of her lady's techniques, positions and nuances, committing to memory what advice she would offer for improvement after the girl had regained her breath and sense following yet another shattering orgasm.

A deep boom from somewhere beyond the ship caught the nun's attention. While the girl desperately steam-pistoned herself, Adelaide listened to an eerie, shrieking noise growing louder and closer, diving in dissonant glissando from high pitch to low.

The crash of iron against the wood hull shook the mighty ship as if God had slapped at a toy boat in the bath.

Ravenna sat up in confusion, her forelocks plastered to her face with sweat, the phallus half submerged, and gasped, "Did I do that?"

From beyond the door the two women heard the panicked cries of the sailors as they ran from prow to stern shouting angry orders.

"To port! To port she comes! Below and man the cannons ya dogs!"

Adelaide hurried to the door, opened it and ran out to the quarterdeck in time to see the blur of an iron ball as it splintered one of the mainsail yard arms, sending the massive spar crashing to the deck and crushing a man beneath its weight.

The first officer appeared, blood trickling from a scalp wound and his eyes wild with panic. He pushed Adelaide back into the room muttering curses and prayers.

"Stay within!" he shouted, "he's still a way off and we may yet prevail, but you must lock yourselves away in case he boards us!"

Ravenna smoothed down her skirts and collected herself enough to ask, "In case *who* boards us?"

"None other than the rapacious bastard himself, m'lady. Noxious Knox Bloodworthe, the Scourge of the Seaways!"

"Saint Salacious, preserve us!" prayed Adelaide, hand to her heart.

"Bolt the door, ladies, and let none enter until we have achieved victory!"

With those words the officer ran off barking orders to his scattered crew.

Adelaide slammed shut the door, twisted the iron key in the lock and secured it in her habit pocket. She turned to her lady with the wide, watery eyes of sheer terror.

Denied the satisfaction of her finish, Ravenna laid the now honey-slicked limestone lingam into its resting place, pulled her long, sweat-wetted hair away from her face and said to her matron, "The officer did say *rapacious*, did he not?"

Chapter 2 - Enter the Pirate, Sans Rapine

For an hour, Ravenna and Adelaide cowered behind the locked door of their cabin as the pirate ship *Black Jaguar* and the *Bentley* met in battle.

Gunpowder smoke burned their nostrils and the ship reared and shook each time the heavy guns hurled iron back at the foe. Men shouted orders and oaths. The wounded screamed for the ship's doctor and the dying for their long dead mothers.

A hit from the *Jaguar* crashed through the hull near the waterline making the boat shudder and reel like an injured animal. The women screamed and held tight to each other on the downy bed.

The sea rushed through the wound and into the lower holds, making the *Bentley* begin to list dangerously to port. The cannons went silent, unable to aim above the water line. Too wounded to return fire and lacking half her sails, the corvette could neither run nor fight.

In the eerie quiet that followed, the women heard the shrill cries of frightened men screaming, "Yonder she comes! Prepare for boarding!"

Musket and pistol fire crackled as the *Jaguar* approached, close enough now that the women could hear the screams and shouts of men from both ships. A great thud and skidding announced the pirate ship had closed abeam and the scraping of grappling hooks and boarding planks against the wood gave way to a mighty roar of the crazed attackers as they poured over the rails.

Ringing steel on steel echoed like pealing church bells as the remaining *Bentley* crew met the boarders in close quarters. Shrieks and death throes rose and fell as the pirates gained the upper hand.

A pair of fighters locked in mortal combat suddenly approached the door, one man grunting in effort, the other laughing through labored gasps as they flailed at each other with their cutlasses. One man thudded against the door and the women held their breath as they heard the laughing man chop his defeated foe's flesh, the blade cracking into bone once, twice, and thrice.

The dying man whimpered his last. A rivulet of dark red blood snaked under the door and into the room. Ravenna watched it with horrified fascination as Adelaide turned away and choked.

The victor grunted a last laugh, spat, and ran off to kill again or die in the attempt.

The women heard a great victory cheer rise from the attackers while the gasping final exhales of the *Bentley* sailors faded away.

A new voice rose over the others, loud, deep, and commanding. Ravenna was sure she was hearing the voice of the Devil himself.

"Hurry you dogs! Bring me the captain or first mate, or any officer still living! You! Red! Take men to the holds and carry what you can to the *Jaguar*!"

The voice reached into Ravenna's belly, stirring and heating a concoction of fear and fascination she had never known.

As the men scattered to the holds and the bridge, the women heard the heavy steps of the man approach the door. They saw his shadow fall over the threshold as he let out a dark laugh and rumbled, "Not feeling well, are we, mate?"

A fresh wave of blood poured under the door as he dragged the mangled corpse away. When he stood before the door again, he waited silently for a moment.

Then, a simple knock on the wood, three quiet raps as deferent and polite as a suitor come calling to his beloved's home.

"Hello?" he sang, his words now delicate and high pitched, "anyone to home?"

As if against her will, Ravenna cleared her throat, making ready to speak. Adelaide slapped her bony hand over the girl's mouth and hissed like a teakettle. They met eyes and the nun shook her head. Ravenna relented, and they held each other tighter.

"Now, now" said the polite gentleman, "let's not be discourteous. I know you are within, Lady Ravenna, and I've come a far distance just to make your acquaintance. Won't you let me in?"

Ravenna's pale cheeks colored deep rose red and her breathing grew shallow and fast, but she made no sound.

"Oh dear, that is disappointing. And here I would think you much better bred and raised than to ignore the reasonable request for your company from a great admirer of your beauty, charm, and wit."

Ravenna smiled. Adelaide pinched her arm, making her jump and grunt a muffled cry of pain.

"Don't fall for his wiles, my lady" the nun whispered, "he means you no good."

The girl nodded at her matron and turned back to the door, her breath coming easier but the flush to her skin now painting her throat and cleavage.

They heard a struggling, frightened man dragged closer by a pirate who said, "Here's the purser, sir, last of the ranks. The captain's half headless and the first mate is swinging from the bowsprit."

"Ah, excellent" said that deep and devilish voice, "just the man I need. The man with all the keys."

The officer groaned in pain as he was manhandled by the sailor.

"So, purser, give me the key to this door and you will die quickly."

"But, but, but" stammered the petty officer.

The fleshy thud of a mighty blow made the man grunt and groan in pain. The women heard him gasp and choke as the leader slammed him against the door and boomed, "Delay, and I will have my men spit roast you alive over an open fire!"

The desperate man searched his ring, the keys clanking and rattling against the door as he tried one, then another, before he took another clouting from the bellowing devil.

"Stall me, purser, and your death will be measured in hours, not seconds!"

The officer was now sobbing and babbling as he again tried one key that failed to unlock the door.

On his next attempt, the key did its work and slipped the iron bolt back from the catch.

The door swung slowly open, creaking on rusted hinges, revealing a tableau that stole the women's breath.

The purser stood gaping with surprise into the darkened room, his blue coat bloodstained and torn, his face a mass of grotesque purple bruises and ragged cuts.

Behind him stood a man so much taller than the doorway that Ravenna could not see his face. His legs, booted to the knee and clothed in black trousers, stood in stark contrast to a coat of blood red with black lapels that framed a billowing shirt of dazzling white silk, spattered with the blood of victims. His left hand, big as a bear paw, held the trembling officer by the shoulder. In his right, he gripped a cutlass dagger long as his forearm.

A handful of curious pirate sailors crowded behind their leader, grinning and laughing as they strained to catch a glimpse of the lady within.

The captain clutched the purser by the hair and yanked his head backward, then slowly drew the thin-edged blade of his dagger across the man's throat.

Adelaide again turned away and sobbed, but Ravenna watched the horrid scene as the man gurgled and coughed his last breath through the open wound. The bright red blood spurted and sprayed onto the door's threshold, making the man's kicking feet slip in the gore as the devil behind held him upright like a marionette.

Finally, as the doomed sailor twitched his last, the captain let him fall.

"Drag off this bucket of bait" he rumbled at his mates, "and toss it to the fishes where it belongs."

The men hurried to do his bidding, taking the chance to cast leering grins at Ravenna, still seated on the bed, breathless and staring, hand at her throat.

When they were gone, the captain ducked his head and stepped through the doorway.

Ravenna stood and faced the man, more giant than man. She gazed wide-eyed and open-mouthed like an opium eater in a belladonic haze, at his face.

Dark as mahogany, regal as a lion, framed by long dreadlocks and a wide, backward tricorne, his eyes burned into hers with volcanic intensity. He smiled broad and white, his mouth rimmed by short, black whiskers, a smile that promised cruelty and compassion in equal measure.

Doffing his hat, he bowed low but held her gaze and said, his deep voice now dripping with the treacle of a diplomat, "The Lady Ravenna Ferdinand, it is my extreme pleasure to make your acquaintance."

Ravenna bowed her head and curtsied.

The captain straightened and began to speak, "I am- "

"Noxious Knox Bloodworthe" Ravenna said, "The Scourge of the Seaways."

The dazzling smile returned. "At your service, lady, though that preamble is not what I would choose for myself."

"No?"

"No, and I believe that, after you have spent some time in close company with me, you will find I am not so... noxious after all."

Adelaide recovered, stood and threw daggers from her eyes at the pirate captain. "Nasty, perhaps?" she snarled. "Nauseating? Noisome?"

Knox laughed, the timbers shuddering with the deep vibrations. "And what is the name of your little pet with the large vocabulary, m'lady?"

"I am Sister Adelaide, Lady Ravenna's companion and protector, and you will not touch her with your filthy, blood-stained hands, or God, through the agency of Saint Salacious, will strike you down where you stand, thou elvish-mark'd, abortive, rooting hog!"

The man considered the sister's words, nodding his head and stroking his chin. "Saint Salacious, you say? I've heard of your order, dear sister. Well, here I give my word to you and to the lady that I will not take a man's pleasure of her delicate flesh, on my honor as a gentleman."

"You won't?" gasped Ravenna.

"I swear on the watery grave of my mother."

Ravenna's face dropped as she looked away and quietly said, "Oh."

"I'll be with her at all times" declared Adelaide, "to see that you don't, thou plague sore."

"I assure you, dear sister, I have no desire to deprive the lady of her virginity."

"You don't?" asked Ravenna.

"No. You are far too valuable to me intact than otherwise. I will ransom you to your father, and he will only pay if he knows you are not... damaged goods."

"The lady is betrothed to the Captain Ozymandias Wembleye" Adelaide said, "and bound to be married the day after tomorrow. You will return her to her father as virginal as she stands here now, or I will cut your heart out myself."

"Oh, I know of her betrothal" the dark pirate said, his smile now slanting sly, "and I am counting on Duke Argo to send the good captain to her rescue."

Ravenna said, "why?"

"Because dear lady" Knox said, bowing slightly, "for his past crimes I must take my revenge upon him, slowly, and with great pain."

"But" Ravenna said, "In the meantime, no raping?"

"No, good lady."

Again she cast her eyes to the floor, her frown deepening. "Oh, dear."

Chapter 3 - Rub-A-Dub-Dub, A Tug in a Tub

As Knox Bloodworthe was securing his victory over the *Bentley*, slaughtering its crew and carrying off Ravenna and Adelaide, Royal Captain Ozymandias Wembleye was ensconced in his quarters, enjoying his third bath of the day.

Having long served Duke Argo in the defense of Hudson and in successful pursuit of brigands, smugglers and spies, Captain Oz, as his men called him, had become a legend throughout the kingdom of Edselfell. King Kaiser-Frazer appointed him Admiral of the Royal Fleet, charged with the coastal protection of all three dukedoms, Hudson, Packard and Tucker. His commission carried with it a generous stipend, apartments in Duke Argo's castle, servants to cater to his every need and the most opulent bathroom facilities in the land.

Naked save for his everyday bicorne hat, Oz splashed happily in the enormous porcelain tub while three serving maids scurried in and out with freshly heated water, soaps, scents and sponges, giggling and making eyes at the man who never glanced their way.

Suds to his chin, he pushed half a dozen toy boats about in the water and muttered a tune he'd learned as a boy.

Rum-te-piddly, piddly rum,
Thrum the iddly-diddily drum.
Hum the melody, don't be glum,
Come and iddly-diddle your chum.
Strum your buddy-boy's piddley plum,

And thumb his iddly-diddly bum.
Thrum the iddly-diddily drum,
Rum-te-piddly, piddly rum.

His first mate, Bilge, short and round and cheery faced, entered and shooed off the girls, chiding them with good natured threats.

"Off with you, nasty li'l cherubs, or I'll have your sweet favors then cook you for m'supper! Our mighty captain's as good as married now and has no eye for the likes of you little temptresses. Off, I say!"

The maids laughed and made rude noises and gestures at the rotund sailor in the white pants and blue jacket, escaping while he did his best to pinch a nipple or pat a fanny.

"Ah, gramercy, dear Bilge" said the captain, "the little sprites were beginning to annoy with their constant chittering and chattering."

"At'cher service, Captain Wembleye, sir."

"Oh, Bilge, we're alone, you needn't stand on such formality."

"Aye, Cap'n Oz."

The pale-skinned man grinned, his chiseled cheeks taking color. "That's better."

"Time for a back-scrubbin' is it sir?"

"Oh, yes please, dear Bilge, you've come at just the right time."

Bilge took up a large, stiff-bristled brush and strapped it to his hand while Oz leaned forward and smiled with anticipation. As the manservant scrubbed his back vigorously, Oz made gurgling and cooing sounds of delight.

"Oh, my, yes dearest Bilge. Mmm, like that, oh yes!"

"Who knows how to care for your groomin' cap'n?"

"Oh, my, you do, dear Bilgey!"

The sailor smiled and scrubbed harder. "'Tis true, I do at that."

"You must teach the Lady Ravenna your techniques, Bilge, since I will soon be forced to give over your company for hers."

"I'd be obliged and honored to do so, cap'n. The happy day approaches, fast as a schooner under full sail."

"Yes. Ravenna is due in port this evening, and the day after tomorrow we will be wed."

Bilge slowed his scrubbing, noticing a change in his master's happy tone. "You don't sound like a man in sharp anticipation of wedded bliss, sir."

"Oh, I am keen to have the dear girl for my own, Bilge, don't hear me wrong. But, well, blast it all, my whole life will be utterly and irreversibly changed, will it not?"

"Aye, sir, that's a truth."

"As I am today I am whole, free to do as I please, to go where I please. And that will end. I will have a wife to cherish, to love and provide for. Perhaps children in time as well, and their needs will drive my work and my care."

Bilge scrubbed more gently and merely nodded.

"I've known only the life of the sea, and I have loved that life, dear Bilge. It's a man's life in the navy, a life of adventure and excitement, of new vistas and old ways."

"The cap'n speaks truth. 'Tis the only life I've known, and the only life I'll ever have."

"I envy you that, Bilge."

"Don't sir, 'tis a lonely life as you well know. Mates aboard ships are but passing phantoms, not family obliged and willin' to be at your back when the wind shifts. If you chance to find a real comrade, a friend true and blue, well then he dies in battle, or is hanged for thievin', or takes another billet, and there you are again, alone and sad."

"I suppose you are right about that. But you have been my dearest friend since I was a boy, and I am loathe to leave you behind."

"I share the sentiment, cap'n. But a wife must be the best friend to her husband, and he to her, and there's no room for a third in between."

"More's the pity."

Bilge waited a moment, trading the brush for a soft sponge and squeezing warm water to rinse the captain's skin. "You love the lass, do you not?" he said.

"Oh yes, Bilge, I do. She is a gem, a rare flower. We spent many wonderful hours together in courtship, before she left for the required year in convent. She has charm and wit, and a ready laugh, and she doted upon me as if I were the very object of her eye."

"Ah, 'tis wonder to behold such love, sir."

"Yes, but most of all, she is so modest and chaste, as becomes a gentlewoman. Do you know, I once made bold to kiss her? She blushed and turned, allowing me only the lightest peck upon her rosy, porcelain-smooth cheek. It was then I knew she was for me. A proper woman to become a proper wife, one who will never act as a wanton wench, rutting and demanding of sexual congress at all times. She will be prim and proper and chaste of character, even during the act of love itself, which we will share for the first time, as two virgins. We are a match as perfect as perfect can be."

As he spoke, the captain laid back in the tub. Bilge continued to squeeze warm water from the sponge, now over his shoulders and chest.

Remembering his encounters with the Lady Ravenna, her beauty and grace, Oz's voice grew quiet, and his gaze hovered out the nearby window. Beyond the opened portal, the late afternoon sun warmed the garden, where the birds were singing, and the sea breeze swayed the branches of the duke's favored lemon trees.

Bilge watched as his captain's manhood, grown hard and long from the reveries of his beloved, peeked above the soapy surface of the bath water.

He said, "Er, beggin' your pardon, cap'n, but would you be in need of one last tug-out 'afore you are married and the duty of relieving you falls upon your lady?"

"Oh yes, Bilge, please. I ache for desire of my Ravenna, but self-abuse is a sin in the eyes of God, as you know. Will you please help me, as you have all these years, perhaps this one last time?"

"Of course, my captain."

Bilge took up a bottle of the thickest scented soap and poured a heavy coating on his hands. Oz lifted himself so his cock and balls were above the water line and closed his eyes. Bilge took to his task, as he had since his charge was a boy, grasping the captain's member in one hand and stroking firmly, squeezing his scrotum with the other and singing a happy song.

Rum-te-piddly, piddly rum,
Thrum the iddly-diddily drum.

Oz smiled and sighed, rocking his pelvis with his man's strokes, his face blushing with the rising heat of his blood.

Hearing the song they knew so well, the serving girls gathered at the open door and watched, grinning brightly and stifling their quiet laughter.

Bilge squeezed harder as he worked the now rigid cock expertly, rolling the balls like dice in a gambler's hand, keeping pace with the tune.

Hum the melody, don't be glum,
Come and iddly-diddle your chum.

"Oh!" gasped Oz, his eyes clenched shut, "Oh, my darling Bil... my Ravenna, my dear, yes!"

The laughter of the serving girls quieted, replaced with sighing breaths of heated desire. One girl hugged her companion from behind, kissing her ear. The third leaned against the other two, watching the men with glowing eyes and squeezing her breasts through her simple cotton bodice.

The manservant's secondary onanism now increased in strength and speed, slapping against the water with each downstroke, drawing a breathy gasp from Oz as he firmly pulled the cock head at the apogee of the cycle. His voice grew louder and gruff as he sang.

Strum your buddy-boy's piddley plum,
And thumb his iddly-diddly bum!

The girls were now awkwardly fondling each other and themselves, fighting to quiet their giggles and groans of pleasure.

Oz thrust his hips as high as he could, grunting now with anticipatory joy, "Oh, my! Oh, my!"

As he belted out the song's coda, Bilge roughly pumped his fist and took firm grip of the balls, pressing a finger hard into his captain's taint, singing loudly.

Thrum the iddly-diddily drum,
Rum-te-piddly, piddly rum!

On the last *rum*, Bilge stopped and squeezed the phallus at the base, still compressing Oz's balls and his root chakra, knowing his master well enough to expertly bring him to climax within the few simple verses of the tune.

Oz held his breath a beat, then let out a high-pitched wail of "Oh, *myyyyy!*"

His spunk ejected with the force of a cannon shot, the first jet rising more than a foot into the air.

The girls gasped, their hands now squeezing and poking each other with abandon.

The captain thrust his hips in rapid rhythm, grunting incoherently as the great ropy arcs of cum rose and fell, lower with each spurt, flowing over Bilge's knuckles like the ejecta of a volcano.

Bilge took to clutching and releasing his captain's cock, pumping out the last of Oz's creamy man butter.

"There's a good lad" he crooned. "Get it all out now. We never leave a *sea-man* behind, do we, sir?"

Oz laughed weakly at the old joke and lowered himself back down into the water, his smile broad and his eyes gazing happily on his oldest and most trusted friend.

"No, dear Bilge, we never leave the *sea-men* behind."

The first mate laughed and released Oz's now withering tadger. As he washed his hands in the soapy water, a commotion started up from the stairwell outside the door.

"Captain Wembleye! Captain Wembleye! You are summoned by the duke!"

The serving girls released one another and smoothed their skirts down as an officer of the duke's guard appeared at the top of the stairs and burst unbidden into the captain's private bath chamber.

"Captain! The duke summons you to the great hall! A terrible tragedy has transpired, and you are needed forthwith!"

Oz regarded the man as he would a barking dog and demanded, "What is so terrible that it requires the interruption of my most necessary ablutions?"

"That blackguard, Noxious Knox Bloodworthe, sir!"

"Bloodworthe? What of him? I've bested him on more than one occasion, and now even my most inexperienced commander can reign in his feeble attempts at piracy."

"A man of his arrived just this moment and delivered a message to the duke. Knox has attacked the *Bentley*."

"The *Bentley*? Hmm. Well, if he's become so bold again, I will attend to him myself. But first, I am in need of a fresh bath. I've somewhat... spoiled this one."

"But captain! That ship was carrying the Lady Ravenna home from Packard! Knox has her and demands all the duke's wealth in gold and goods for her safe return!"

Oz stood in the tub, suds not quite obscuring his supine prick, making the officer blanch and turn away.

The girls in the doorway strained to get a better look.

"He has Ravenna?" Oz shouted, "the soulless bastard! I'll tear his heart out and feed it to the fish! I'll tie him to the prow of my ship to make his bleached bones my figurehead!"

"The duke awaits you, captain" the officer said, still turned away, "along with the messenger from the pirate to carry back your answer."

"And answer him I will" Oz growled, low and menacing, "but first, I really do need at least a quick shower."

The officer said, "A shower? Now?"

"Yes. Bilge? Body wash and sponge!"

"Aye, cap'n!"

"Girls! Bring your watering cans! And quickly!"

Chapter 4 - We Might as Well Get It Over With

From the quarterdeck of the Black Jaguar, Ravenna and Adelaide stood by Captain Knox and watched the *Bentley* burn as it listed deeper into the sea with every passing minute.

The crackling red blaze mirrored the setting sun and filled the sky with smoke black as midnight. The sails flashed red, and gold then disappeared, and finally the flag of Hudson at the top of the main mast burst into flame, its final wisps of soot carried away on the evening breeze.

Knox laughed and pointed, saying, "Now Duke Argo must meet my demands and turn over all his earthly wealth before he ever again lays eyes on his beautiful daughter."

A clutch of pirates surrounded the trio, all but one gawking and leering at the young lady. One pirate, short, old and wizened but still muscled, with a sideways bicorne hat and an ivory pipe clamped in his mouth, instead cast his gaze on the nun, waggling his eyebrows and winking at her.

She pulled her veil tight around her wrinkled face, grimaced and threw him a two-fingered salute.

Dabbing at her tears with a kerchief, Ravenna said, "All his earthly wealth?"

"Yes, pretty one. It is my intent to rob your father into penury, to empty his vaults of every last ducat. He will be unable to pay his creditors, his guards or his taxes. When the king learns this he will

23

surely seize the duke's lands and leave him scrabbling in the dust for his daily bread."

Ravenna gaped at the dark man and whined, "But, why?"

"I have my reasons!" he screamed; his face now wild. "What has been stolen from me will be returned a hundred-fold!"

Adelaide said, "Captain Oz will defeat you before you can realize your evil plans, thou rampallian."

Watching the sinking Bentley, the last of the flames flickering in the pirate's eyes, he whispered, "We shall see about that."

Knox broke from his reveries and shouted at his crew, "Avast, you mangy sea dogs and other pirate-y curses! Away with you and to your tasks, or you'll beg for death after a keel hauling! Begone!"

The men scattered, yelling orders and oaths.

Knox pointed to the man with the pipe. "Squid, take the nun and lock her in your cabin. You'll bunk in berthing for the duration."

"Aye cap'n"

Adelaide pulled away from the man's grasp and shouted, "You said I would stay with the lady, to watch over her, thou rankest compound of villainous smell that ever offended nostril!"

"I made no such promise, little nun. And I'll thank you to keep your place. Neither God nor the Devil rules here. The Black Jaguar is my ship, and every soul aboard is either my crewman or my prisoner, so you'll do as you're told. Take her away, Squid."

The officer obeyed his captain and dragged Adelaide away roughly as she screamed oaths in an ancient language known only to the Sisters of Saint Salacious but sounding very much like *fuck your fucking fuck, you fuck!*

As the nun's shouts faded away, Ravenna asked, "And what of me?"

"You, my dear, will take my cabin." He held his arm out like a gentleman at a cotillion inviting the lady to dance.

Ravenna glanced at his offered arm, then met his eyes. "And if I refuse?"

"Then I will tie you to the mainmast, where you will weather the night."

"I despise you, for you are a killer and a thief and a liar."

"I am, indeed, all those things."

She laid her hand over his. "But you are the captain of this ship. And so I will obey."

His smile grew broad and white, his eyes now reflecting the last reddish glow of the setting sun. "This way, m'lady."

Knox led Ravenna past the great wheel to his spacious cabin in the stern of the ship.

Inside the dining cabin, she gaped in wonder at the richly appointed room, large enough for a long dining table in the center, with intricately embroidered tapestry rugs and upholstered chairs of polished mahogany. Candelabras and ewers of jewel-encrusted gold cluttered every side table. Knox led her through the next set of doors to his day cabin. The many windows along the back wall glowed with the setting sun. Knox left Ravenna at the threshold and went to his navigation table near the windows. He consulted a map, then shouted for his ship master.

A man burst through the door and stopped short, seeing Ravenna. He grinned at her, then saluted. "Yes, captain?"

"Steer her south-east and spill the wind. We need not travel fast or far."

"Aye sir!" The man gave the lady one last oily grin and hurried through the door.

Ravenna strolled the length of the room, her delicate fingers running along the glass-like sheen of the dark wood table. "Hudson is the other direction. You are running away?"

"Not running, lady. Merely choosing where I will set my trap for your Captain Oz."

"He has defeated you before. He will this time as well."

Knox took a bottle from the table, uncorked it and began filling two golden goblets. "The gods of the sea are a fickle lot, but I will not fail to defeat him, this time. I will kill his crew, rob his ship of everything down to its nails, sink it, and personally, slowly and with immense pleasure, send him to the Abyss."

He held out a goblet. "Wine, m'lady?"

She reached him and took it, glancing into the dark liquid. "What makes you so certain?"

"You do."

"Me?"

"Your dear captain will know you are aboard this ship. How do you think that knowledge will affect his plans for battle?"

Ravenna felt the blood rush from her head.

"Your pale lips" he said, "tell me you understand the situation. He will hesitate, will order minimal bombardment, will use every skill and trick at his disposal to attack without endangering your life, the life that is precious to him, perhaps more precious than even his own soft, scented and well moisturized skin. You will be his undoing."

Ravenna waited a moment to regain her composure and said, "Even for all that disadvantage, he will be victorious, and I will watch with great pleasure as you are hanged, by the neck as the saying goes, until you are dead."

The dazzling smile returned. "You are living proof, dear Ravenna, that every man and woman harbors a pirate's heart just under the carefully crafted mask with which we face the world. For all your feigned delicate nature, girlish wiles and preposterously long blond hair, there is a woman locked deep inside you who longs to cut a throat and taste the blood from her blade."

She felt the heat rise in her cheeks and saw the captain enjoy the sight of her discomfort.

"A woman" he continued, "who has many ravenous appetites she aches to satisfy, if the wind would but shift and take her in a direction she did not realize she wished to go."

After a moment, she said, "My only wish is to be reunited with my beloved Oz, marry him, and be the lady of his household, as is my birth and breeding."

The pirate's laugh reached into her belly and lit a small fire. "Well, that's as may be. But I drink to that other woman, smiling at me from behind your eyes."

He lifted his goblet in salute.

She lifted hers and said, "I drink to Captain Ozymandias Wembleye, and to your imminent demise."

"As you wish" Knox said and quaffed his wine.

She sipped hers and set the goblet on the table.

Walking slowly toward a velvet cushioned day bed against the near wall, she said, "Since I know you are, among other things, an inveterate liar, I suppose now is the time when you break your oath to Sister Adelaide and rape me."

She sat on the bed and laid back against the angled headboard, arranging her skirts and fluffing her ridiculously shiny golden hair over her shoulders.

"We might as well get it over with" she said.

The dark captain set his goblet down, took off his tricorne and laid it on the map table. He stood and went to the bed, towering over her and smiling at her now flushed face and determined stare.

"No."

"No?" she gasped.

"As I said before, I have no intention of taking your virginity." He squinted at her and said, "You are a virgin, are you not?"

"Yes. Well, technically."

"Technically?"

"No man has ... has ..."

"Fucked you?"

She gasped at the word and the flush colored her from forehead to cleavage.

"N-no. But I've ... well, I've used, you see ..."

The captain's eyes widened, and he smiled more brightly. "Ah, yes, I remember now. The convent of the Sisters of Saint Salacious. You've been there for a year before your wedding."

She broke from his gaze. "Yes."

"So you've had your petals parted by a penile substitute."

"Um ..."

"But you have not" he said, his tone lowering, "had a man, a man who stares into your eyes as he lays you down ..."

Ravenna's eyes glistened into the captain's as he spoke.

"... who kisses you, gently at first, perhaps, but then deeper and harder as his blood heats."

"No" she whispered.

"A man who, for a time, fights down the demons rising in his loins, who struggles to hold you softly and tenderly ..."

Ravenna's gaze began lowering from his eyes to his mouth, to his throat, to the tops of his pectoral muscles visible over the open collar of his white shirt, the deep brown skin gleaming with sweat in the flickering lantern light.

"... but who cannot long keep the beast within chained, and finally tears at your clothes to claim your breasts, your legs, your sweet, wet cunny ..."

Her eyes reached his belt buckle, then lower, wondering what hid in those black trousers of rough fabric. Her hands went to her breasts without her permission, lifting them and pressing, her cleavage rising like bread dough, her breath becoming shallow.

"... and who finally holds you down by your shoulders as he growls and forces his ramrod cock deep into your waiting, aching flesh!"

"No!" she cried, "no, I've not had that, I've not, oh God!"

Knox grinned. "Nor shall you."

Ravenna shook her head as if waking from a dream. "What?"

"I told you. I've no intention of enjoying your pretty pleasures."

"But, but ... you're Knox Bloodworthe!"

"That I am, good lady."

"The thieving, murderous, *rapacious* Scourge of the Seaways!"

He bowed. "Again, at your service."

"But you won't rape me?"

"No."

"Not even ... a little?"

"I've told you, I need you intact to achieve my ends. And besides, virgins bore me. Even technical ones."

He turned and walked toward the door. "You'll be locked away here until I trade you back to your father. I'll have my cook bring you supper."

His hand on the door latch, Ravenna shouted, "Wait!"

He turned and smiled. "Yes?"

"I don't suppose you have anything aboard that, well, that could serve as, as a..."

He laughed. "As a substitute?"

"Yes."

"Hmm. Not that I know of, but this is a motley crew from many lands. Perhaps I can find something suitable."

"About this long?" She held her hands apart.

"Really?"

"Yes, and about like this?" She made a ring with her thumb and forefinger.

"Hmm, impressive. Seems you've been ... practicing at an elevated level. I'd say your virginity is indeed technical."

His eyes drank her in from her insanely long blond hair to her delicate feet.

"I'll see what I can find."

He stepped through the door. Ravenna heard him use the key to throw the latch and walk away.

She closed her eyes, tugged the hem of her skirt up and breathed an oath, "Saint Salacious, help me in my hour of need."

Chapter 5 - Laughing Pirate, Killer Nun

Squid opened the door to his tiny cabin and pushed the struggling nun over the threshold.

"I'll cut your balls off with a rusty blade!" she screamed, "and feed them to the dogs, thou hedge-pig, thou bow-case, thou vile standing tuck!"

The sailor followed her in and shut the door. "Right nasty tongue for one who's taken the vows."

"My vows don't keep me from knowing evil when I see it, and calling it by name, thou quailing maggot-pie."

"Now, now sister, fret not. Your lady will suffer no harm from Knox, and neither will you, I give my word."

The little nun scoffed a laugh. "Your word? The word of a scoundrel, lap dog to a worse scoundrel. Pah! Shove your word right up your dankish bum-baily for what it's worth."

Adelaide walked unsteadily to a small table of rough wood in the center of the room and sat in a chair, groaning in rheumatic discomfort.

Squid smiled and tapped his pipe out against the table leg. "Believe me or not, I tell ye I know my cap'n, an' if he says he'll not harm the lady, then his word's his bond and he'll not break it."

Adelaide rubbed her aching knees and grumbled, "And what of you, foot-licker?"

Squid took a pinch of tobacco from a gold-gilt box on the table and stuffed his pipe. "What of me?"

"Is the captain's first mate a man of his word?"

"An' who says I'm the first mate?"

"This room" Adelaide waved to the bare walls and rickety cot. "Apart from the captain, only the first mate gets his own cabin."

Squid smiled, lighting a taper from the lamp on the table. "Well, now, here's a wonder. A nun who knows something of sailorin.' I thought the only things ye Sisters of Saint Salacious did all day was pray and take yer pleasure of carved cocks."

"That is the training for brides-to-be." Adelaide smoothed her habit's tunic over her legs and loosened the veil, growing warmer in the small room. "The sisters are scholars and teachers. We help young ladies prepare for the rigors of marriage, but we deprive ourselves of all pleasures, giving over all worldly pursuits in the service of God."

Squid was lighting and puffing his pipe. He exhaled a billowing cloud and laughed. "My my, there's a pity. Helping beautiful maidens to pound their pretty pussies with pretend pricks, and none for yerselves? Ye serve a cruel God, ye do."

Adelaide wrinkled her nose and waved to clear the smoke. "I wish I'd had training at the convent before my marriage, I can tell you."

"So? Married were ye?"

"Yes. A sailor. But not for long. He died young."

"At sea?"

"No. I killed him."

The old salt raised his eyebrows and let out a puff of smoke.

Adelaide gave him a sneering grin. "I cut off his balls and fed them to the dog."

Squid burst into laughter, staggering about the cabin and slapping his knees. He laughed his way into a coughing fit and fell on the cot gasping for breath as he wiped his teary eyes.

"Gods of the deep!" he croaked, finally catching his wind, "I am in the company of a true goddess! A pious nun teaching girls how to fuck their husbands after killing her own!"

He lay on the cot holding his belly and chuckling.

Adelaide's lips turned upward slightly. "Well, he was a bastard who deserved it."

"All men are bastards who deserve it, dear woman, an' you know that as well as I do."

Adelaide regarded the laughing sailor with raised eyebrows. "You're the first man I've ever heard say it."

He sat up, pulled a dirty rag from his pocket and wiped his face. "Of course we can't say it, but we all know it, somewhere deep in our black, condemned souls."

Adelaide felt her cheeks warm and looked away. "Maybe not all."

"Oh? Name one. I dare ye."

"I believe Captain Ozymandias, Ravenna's betrothed, to be a good man."

Squid laughed again. "Oh? Met Captain Oz, have ye?"

"No, but the lady has spoken highly of him the entire year of her cloister. And he writes her the most beautiful love letters."

"Dear Sister Adelaide, I would expect a woman with guts enough to castrate her own husband to know better. Every man will break his beloved's heart. He'll do it when she's young, as I suspect yours did, or he'll do it many years after the vows are spoken. But break her heart he will. The only difference is this, does the lady forgive and stay, or kill him in his sleep?"

Adelaide kept her eyes down on the floor. "He wasn't asleep. I watched the life leave his eyes."

Squid laughed again. "Yer in the wrong business, sister. If ye'd like to sign on to the *Jaguar*, I'll give Cap'n Knox my personal recommendation."

"Thank you, but no. I answer to a power higher than any captain. And I have dedicated my life to helping young women prepare for marriage, so as to avoid the... difficulties I faced."

"And do ye teach the girls the great truth I just uttered? That all men are bastards and will break their hearts?"

Adelaide hesitated. "No."

"Then ye do them a great disservice. If ye think to prepare them for marriage without revealing what every woman should know before she grows tits, ye cannot call yourselves teachers and scholars."

Adelaide faced Squid with angry eyes. "We teach them to care for themselves, their bodies, minds, and hearts, and to demand of any husband that they be treated as equals and given the ability to live the life they want. Don't you dare say we fail in our holy mission!"

"If the lass isn't ready for that heartbreak, she'll never get over it, and will live a life of despair. Or like you, she'll kill the husband. Then she's alone and in despair, and the poor bastard himself didn't get the chance to repent and learn to become a whole man. You do a double disservice, sister."

The nun and the sailor sat glaring into each other's eyes until they heard heavy footsteps approaching. Captain Knox threw open the cabin door and ducked under the lintel.

"I've a task for you, mate."

Squid stood and saluted. "Aye cap'n?"

"The Lady Ravenna has been deprived of something she treasures. I need you to find something suitable as a replacement."

"An' what's that, sir?"

Knox looked at Adelaide and stammered, "She needs... well, she may not need but very much would like... um... well..."

Squid smiled. "A practice cock, cap'n?"

"Aye, yes, um, yes. Do you think you could find something... suitable?"

"And what sort of dimensions, sir? Say, the beam and carlin?"

The captain said, "Carlin of about..." and held his hands apart.

The mate's eyebrows arched. "Aye?"

"And beam perhaps like so." Knox circled his fingers and thumb.

The first mate whistled. "It might take a bit of lookin.' But if nothin's found, I'll carve one myself."

"Good man."

Squid grinned at Adelaide. "Perhaps the good sister will be so kind as to help me in this most important and..." he winked, "urgent mission?"

"Excellent idea." The captain pointed to Adelaide. "You will assist him."

Knox stood a moment, looking at Squid and Adelaide, then said, "Yes," and strode out the door.

Staring into the old sailor's smiling eyes, Adelaide's frown softened as she said, "Bastard."

Squid bowed low and kept the nun's gaze. "At'cher service, ma'am."

Chapter 6 - Clichés
Aweigh!

The red glow of sunset still burned through the windows in the great hall of Duke Argo's castle as servants lighted torches to last the night.

The duke and duchess sat together at the high table awaiting Captain Oz. Gleda, as annoyingly gifted with long, shining, flaxen hair as her daughter, shook with fear and cried quietly, struggling to not break down in front of their household.

Stout, dark-bearded Argo sat stone-faced, staring at the screened passage on the far side of the room.

"Where is that perfumed ponce?" he growled.

"Don't start with the name calling" Gleda said, dabbing at her eyes with a lace handkerchief, "he's your son-in-law after all."

"Not yet, he isn't. And maybe I'll get lucky, and he'll get himself killed rescuing Ravenna."

"Argo! Ravenna loves the man, damn it, and that's all that counts."

"Ha! There's a lot more to a marriage than a naive girl's love, my dear."

The duchess rolled her eyes. "Oh, do tell! As if you're a great expert on the topic."

"You know what I mean. As a sailor and a captain and a pirate hunter, Oz is the best. Beyond that, he's just... a little too interested in moisturizing, if you get my drift."

"There's nothing hidden about your accusations, Argo. You think a fastidious man is homosexual or just not manly enough. You could learn a thing or two from a man who keeps himself so clean."

Argo scoffed, "Clean? Oz is practically sterile. You could eat porridge off his bum without a worry. His hands are softer than Ravenna's, and that's not right. A man should—"

"Stink of dick-cheese, like you?"

Argo eyed his wife with a sneer. "That was only one time, Gleda, one time!"

"Once was enough."

A guard at the passage shouted, "My lord! Captain Ozymandias Wembleye answers your summons."

Argo grumbled, "Finally dragged his ass from the bath, did he?"

Gleda kicked his shin under the table, making the duke grunt in pain and pinch her nipple in reprisal. She squealed and jabbed him hard in the ribs with her knuckles.

The couple were about to start one of their regular slap fights when Oz strode through the passageway, Bilge in tow.

Resplendent in his deep blue tailcoat with gold trim and buttons, white trousers and black boots, Oz called out, "I hurry to your summons, my lord Argo." He reached the high table, doffed his bicorne hat and bowed deeply. "And to Your Grace, beloved Gleda, I offer my regret for the anguish you must be feeling, and my vow to return Ravenna to you safe and unharmed."

Gleda smiled and gestured as she said, "Rise, dear captain. We appreciate your care and have every confidence you will save our girl, your betrothed."

Oz stood, donned his hat and grasped the hilt of the rapier at his side. "My sword, my ship and my life I commit to the task."

Argo shouted at the guards, "Bring in the pirate, the messenger from Knox!"

Two guards led a tall, muscular man through the passage and walked the length of the hall toward the nobles. Typical of seagoing criminals, he wore tall boots and striped trousers, a leather vest over a billowing white shirt, and a sneering smile on his unshaven face. A red bandanna covering his greasy hair and one gold earring finished the picture.

"Lords of the waves" Oz mumbled, "Only a third-rate scribbler of fantastical tales would dress you in such a hackneyed getup."

The pirate's hands were tied, and when the guards stopped him before Oz, he spat on the captain's polished boot.

Oz glanced at the spittle then met the pirate's eye. "You'll come to regret that, you cur."

"An' ye'll come to regret the day you was born when Cap'n Knox guts ye like a fish, ye bum-lickin' Nancy-boy."

Oz tisked. "Predictable lines, as well."

Argo stood and shouted, "Enough! Give him Knox's message, as you told me, and be quick about it. My daughter's life is at stake, and I'll not waste time with the likes of you."

The man grinned like a death's head and bowed slightly, "Of course, Your Grace."

"Well?" said Oz. "Out with it, scum."

"Knox Bloodworthe sends ye all his highest regards, 'specially you, Captain Oz, an' his word that the Lady Ravenna will not be harmed and will be returned to you... intact. But only if the duke hands over his entire treasury, down to the last sou, by sundown tomorrow."

"Do you hear?" Argo blurted, "my entire treasury! I have debts, and taxes due to the king. I'll be ruined!"

Gleda stood and scolded her husband, "Our daughter is worth ten treasuries. Pay the scoundrel and be done with it."

"You'll sing a different tune when we're made serfs under the king's wrath, woman!"

The pirate continued, "An' the great Captain Ozymandias must make delivery personally, but only he and a scant crew. If ye come with a fleet, the girl dies."

"Where am I to meet him?"

"He awaits yer arrival a day's sail sou-east of here."

"I can't give him everything" whined the duke.

"If ye keep so much as a ducat, she dies."

Oz said, "Why so great a ransom? Knox will just be emboldened to do the same to others with wealth."

"He'll not" said the pirate. "With so great a store, the cap'n will retire from piratin' an' live like a king on an uncharted island. He'll be satisfied to know Argo is scrabblin' in the garbage fer food while he drinks fine wine from jewel encrusted goblets."

Argo laughed. "So he says! I'll be undone but he'll keep plundering every nobleman from here to the king."

The pirate shook his head. "No, he's given his word to his mates, an' sends it to ye as well. He's done with the life."

"And if the duke refuses?" asked Oz.

The pirate's broad smile revealed the glistening cliche' of a gold tooth. "After all the scurvy seadogs on the *Jaguar* have had enjoyment of her every hole, we'll throw her to the sharks and laugh as she screams her last."

Gleda shouted, "By God, you will *not*!" She grabbed the jeweled dagger from her husband's belt and came around the table with her eyes on fire.

The pirate laughed heartily and kept on laughing up to the exact moment the duchess drove the dagger under the man's jaw and into the base of his brain.

The surprised victim's last breath spewed a great font of blood on Gleda's face and breasts, while the rest spattered the captain's impeccably starched trousers and polished boots.

Gleda released her hold on the dagger and the pirate slumped to the floor, twitching like a slaughtered hog.

Oz eyed the dead man. "I said you would regret soiling my boots, wretch."

Argo slowly approached his wife, who stood over her quarry breathing heavily through a grin of bloodlust.

"Darling" he whispered, "are you well? How fares my..."

Gleda turned her bloodied face to the captain and growled, "You will bring Ravenna home safe and that bastard Knox to my pleasure. He'll get nothing but what his man got, but more slowly and painfully. Do you hear me?"

"I hear and obey" Oz said, bowing stiffly. "I will sail with this evening's tide, but first..."

Argo frowned. "But first, what?"

"I'll need a bath. I mean, look at me!" He pointed to his trousers and boots. "Spittle and blood? No way for a captain to sport himself."

"You'll go now!" shouted the duchess.

"A quick shower, then."

"Now!" Argo and Gleda screamed in unison.

"Won't take a minute. Bilge? Call the girls."

"Aye cap'n!"

Oz led his man toward the passage, taking great strides as he barked out orders. "Lay out fresh trousers, Bilge, and with these, remember, blot, don't rub."

"Aye sir."

"Just a quick lather, rinse off and powdering should do the trick, I think."

"Agreed, sir!"

As the ablution-addled Oz made his way from the hall, Gleda eyed her husband and said, "You're right. He *is* a ponce."

Chapter 7 - Apple Pie
with Iced Confession

As darkness fell and the stars began their nightly dance, the crew of the *Black Jaguar* furled the sails and dropped the sea anchor, leaving the ship rocking and quietly creaking in the gentle waves of the Plymouth Sea.

Sailors of the night watch took their stations while the rest of the crew caroused on the gun decks below. Profane oaths and songs echoed over the waves as lamplight poured through the gun portals and glowed as golden sparks floating on the ink black water.

Sitting at the long, polished table in the captain's cabin, Ravenna finished a hearty meal of roast beef, bread and ale. Starved since morning, she ate hungrily, losing the gentle table etiquette of her upbringing.

A quiet rapping at the door startled her. She wiped grease from her lips with a kerchief and swallowed a gulp of ale before saying, "Come in?"

Knox entered carrying a tray with a large pitcher, a mug and something covered in a cloth. He kicked the door closed behind him and set the tray on the table.

He nodded at her empty plate. "Enjoying the fare?"

"Yes, very much, thank you."

"It came from the *Bentley*. Before we raided her we were living on salt pork and biscuits."

"The beef was excellently prepared, as if I was at court, not aboard a pirate ship."

Knox smiled. "My cook was once a gourmet chef to a lord in a far-off land. Until he decided he coveted the man's wife enough to poison him and had to flee for his life."

Ravenna grinned. "My complements to the poisoner, then."

Knox chuckled. "More ale?"

"Yes, please." She held out her mug and the captain filled it from the pitcher. "I'd never tasted ale before, and I love it. I've only ever had wine, and not much of that. Ale is delicious."

Knox filled his mug and held it up in salute. "Wine is but single broth, while ale is meat, drink and cloth."

She smiled and saluted. "Here's to ale."

They drank, holding each other's gaze.

Knox pointed to the cloth cover on the tray. "I brought you something else I hope you will enjoy."

Ravenna's eyes brightened and her cheeks flushed. "Is it... did you?"

He lifted the cloth with a flourish, and Ravenna's smile faded.

He grinned proudly. "It's an apple pie. The *Bentley* was carrying a season's crop from Packard. Cook baked it specially for you."

"Oh, well, I do love apple pie." Her voice betrayed her appreciation. "But I did hope, or rather wished..."

"Ah, that. I have my best man on the task. Nothing yet, but I'm sure he and your matron will scare something up soon."

"How is Adelaide? You are caring for her as well as you do for me, are you not?"

"I am, dear lady, fear not. She is safely ensconced in my mate's cabin, just as you are safe from lusting eyes here. Squid and I will bunk in berthing with the crew."

"That is kind of you. I hope we are not a burden."

Knox took a chair. "A burden? No, dear lady. Remember my intentions. You are the key to my treasure house, my golden egg-laying goose. Caring for you is like fattening a prize calf to fetch the best price at market."

"Is that why the beef and apple pie? You are fattening me for the slaughter?"

"In a sense, and because I keep my word. If your father relents and pays your ransom, I will send you home unharmed, untouched, and perhaps better fed than you were during your cloister. Then I will retire and live like a king in peace and seclusion. As to your *slaughter*, well, that will come in the wedding bed at the hands of your husband."

"Captain Oz, you mean."

Knox downed a swallow of ale and shook his head. "No. Oz will not survive our encounter, so he will never be your husband."

Ravenna stared a moment into the frothy ale in her mug. "Do you mean, even if my father sends Oz with all his wealth, you still intend to kill the captain?"

"Whatever the outcome of this adventure, above all else, Oz must die, as slowly and painfully as possible."

"Why do you harbor such enmity for the captain, and for my father?"

Ravenna watched the pirate's dark face in the lamplight, seeing waves of sadness and anger rise and fall.

Finally, he downed his ale and cleared his throat. "Don't concern yourself with it." He offered a sad smile. "Have some pie."

He reached for a knife on the tray, and she gripped his wrist.

"Tell me. I have the right to know why you want to ruin my father and kill my betrothed."

Knox set down the knife, took up the pitcher and filled her mug, then his own. "I suppose you do at that."

Ravenna swallowed a deep draft of the ale, her eyes on Knox.

"You were perhaps too young, or your parents kept matters of state from you."

"I've never cared for court or politics, war or peace. They tried to educate me in such things, but all I wanted to do was play and dream of my future."

The pirate smiled. "Proof we are often smarter as children than when old."

"Go on" she said and took another drink.

He also drank and sighed. "For ten years I was the greatest buccaneer on the Plymouth Sea. Feared and reviled from Tucker to Hudson and beyond. No navy could catch me. No privateer could defeat me. I grew rich and powerful, a king of pirates, and all the best sailors and deadliest cutthroats wanted to serve on my ship."

"I used to read of your exploits in little pamphlets that were handed around the villages, romantic tales of swashbuckling and murder on the high seas."

"Ha! Most of what those rags printed were lies, made up stories, and they were never as bloody and glorious as what the truth was, living a life like mine."

Ravenna took a swallow of her ale, her glistening eyes fixed on the pirate's face.

"During that time, my first mate was the love of my life."

The lady's eyes widened. "You mean, Squid?"

The hearty laugh from Knox rattled the rafters and Ravenna felt it echo within her belly.

"No, not Squid. Bonnie 'Bones' Blondhate, the loveliest, meanest and most blood-thirsty woman I ever set eyes on. Strong as an ox, she was. She could wrestle three swabbies at once and knock them all to their asses. But beautiful and womanly, with pale freckled cheeks and bright red hair, big knockers and skin like a seal."

Ravenna giggled and sipped her ale.

"And laugh? devil of the deep, could Bones laugh and make us laugh. Life itself was one big joke to her. She'd slit a man's throat then purse her lips and squeal, 'Oopsie, he said he wanted a close shave!'"

Knox laughed and drank, and Ravenna joined him in both.

But the man's face grew hard, his eyes mean, and Ravenna watched the muscles in his jaws flex as he ground his teeth before taking a breath to speak again.

"Seven years ago now, your captain Oz took his first command, vowing to your father and the king to rid the seas of pirates, myself at the top of the list. He started harassing us and succeeded. We'd hear of a rival ship burned, sunk and the entire crew sent to the gallows. The captains and mates they gibbeted 'til their bones bleached in the sun."

"I was just a girl. I cared nothing about this."

"As is proper. Children should keep their innocence, the time before learning of men's sins and the hard world that leads them on the path to sin."

Ravenna nodded and sipped her ale.

"Oz fairly cleared the lanes of us. We took to running and hiding, not at ease in any port for the bounties on our heads made every man, woman and child ready to betray our whereabouts. We were half starving, sick and penniless. That's when he set his trap."

"Trap?"

Knox took three deep swallows of ale and rubbed his mouth with the back of his hand. "A sure bet. A gold shipment from Hudson was due in the tiny port town of Muntz. Only a handful of soldiers to guard it for the night and day it would be in the armory. We were hungry and careless and took the bait. There was no gold, only Oz in command of Royal Marines. I took a musket ball to the guts and went down in the first volley. Bones led most of the men to attack as others pulled me out. The last I saw as I went under was her flailing cutlass hacking off arms that fell to the deck with pistols and sabers still in hand."

Ravenna sat unbreathing as the pirate spoke.

"My men got me to our ship and weighed anchor. I lay nearly dying as the surgeon cut the ball out and stopped the bleeding. A night and a day passed before I opened my eyes and heard the news."

"They killed Bones?"

"Not at first. They gunned down most of the men and hanged the rest. But Bonnie, her they decided to make an example as the only woman hung alive in the gibbet."

Ravenna gasped. "I didn't... couldn't..."

"No, and good thing, too. But I had to see her, so I ordered my men to get me to the port at Hudson. She was still alive as we watched from offshore, screaming curses upon all the bastards who ever laid hands on her and crying for water or the sweet taste of death."

Ravenna dropped her face into her hands.

"With only a handful left of my crew, I screamed at them to sail in and rescue her, but the fever overtook me, and again I fell into the well of blackness. When I awoke, she was dead. For the next year I came back and secretly watched her dear, sweet body eaten by crow and fly, her flesh slough off and her bones dry in the midday sun."

Ravenna drew a deep breath through her fingers.

"The plan was from Oz. Argo ordered her murder."

Ravenna sat up and gaped at Knox, eyes red and her rouging cheeks wet with tears.

"So now you know." The pirate finished his ale, slammed the mug on the table and stood. "What has been stolen from me will be returned a hundred-fold."

Ravenna struggled to breathe as she sobbed, "But why not kill me, to get back at them, as they killed her?"

"Because I am a better man than your beloved Oz."

Knox hurried to the door.

"Eat your pie" he said, "before it gets cold."

Chapter 8 - Vortex of Death for Two, Please

Eighteen hours out of port at Hudson, the corvette *LaSalle* struggled against headwinds and choppy seas under full sail to find and engage the *Black Jaguar*. A storm on the horizon an hour before was now upon them, the dark clouds enveloping the sky and blotting out the afternoon sun.

As the ship pitched and rolled and waves crashed over the bow, the sailors rushed about the deck furling and trimming sails to tack a zigzag course south-east, shouting orders and curses. They extinguished cooking fires and lashed cannons to the deck as the swells rose. First Mate Bilge ordered the ship's carpenter to rig lifelines, and quickly a network of taut ropes crisscrossed the deck to avoid losing men overboard when the worst of the storm arrived.

In his cabin, Captain Ozymandias Wembleye splashed happily in a small brass tub of warm water and suds, occasionally losing a toy boat over the side when the ship pitched.

Despite his attention to all things lavatorial, Oz listened carefully to the sea, the wind, the ship and the men. Years as sailor and captain taught him the difference between the sounds of troubled sailing and those of crisis requiring his attention. Hearing only the usual difficulties of encountering a storm at sea, he continued with his ritualistic cleansing, muttering his favorite tune.

Rum-te-piddly, piddly rum,
Thrum the iddly-diddily drum.

Oz happily lathered a cloth with his second-favorite eucalyptus and mint scented soap, then scrubbed his arms and chest for the seventh time.

Hum the melody, don't be glum,
Come and iddly-diddle your chum.

As he was about to employ his back-brush, he stopped singing and listened, hearing a change in the men's chatter. A shout from the crow's nest echoed in many voices, growing louder and shriller.

Bilge burst through the cabin door. "Captain Oz!"

"You've spotted the *Jaguar*."

"Yes sir, off the port bow just at the horizon, her sails struck and waiting."

"Order full speed ahead and battle stations. Overtake the *Jaguar* as quickly as possible."

"Aye, cap'n."

"And Bilge?"

"Yes, sir?"

"Next time, be sure to stow some of my favorite lavender and rosemary soap. This lot is barely serviceable to my needs."

Bilge smiled. "I have three bars tucked away, cap'n. I thought you might wish to save it to celebrate your victory over old Noxious."

"Brilliant, Bilge. Remind me to put you in for a commendation when we conclude this little scuffle."

"All in a day's work, sir."

By the time Captain Oz emerged from his quarters, blue coat and white trousers impeccably pressed, boots polished and bicorne sporting a pheasant quill, the *LaSalle* was a mere quarter mile from the *Jaguar*. The swells had deepened, and the wind had risen, tossing both boats wildly. The *LaSalle* pitched and rolled more violently than the *Jaguar* as the men struggled to keep sail enough the close the distance.

The *Jaguar's* sails remained struck, steadying her in the rough seas.

Oz used his spyglass to sweep a look at the far-off ship's deck. "Hmm. Odd, the quarterdeck looks deserted."

"Men overboard, cap'n?" Bilge surmised.

"More likely a ruse, my dear Bilge. Knox is the sort of scurrilous bastard who would trick a man into taking it up the bum with ne'er a reach-around."

"No honor, that's him sir."

"Indeed." Oz lowered the glass. "Order the crew to close in and cut to starboard, bring the port guns to bear and stand ready."

"Aye sir!"

"And fly the signal flags ordering surrender."

Bilge hurried off shouting orders.

Oz kept his eyes on the enemy boat, whispering to himself, "If I find that one single strand of Ravenna's incredulously long, unsettlingly shiny, impeccably conditioned hair has been so much as mussed out of place, I shall be... very put out."

The distance between the two ships narrowed quickly, the swells now chafed with whitecaps in the howling wind.

Bilge held tight to a lifeline to steady himself as he returned to his captain's side, shouting, "Signals up, sir, and guns ready!"

Oz fought to keep his balance as he raised the spyglass again, watching a man on the *Jaguar* struggle to the stern and run up a series of signal flags. Oz squinted, used a lace-edged hankie to clean both lenses of the scope and looked again.

He handed the instrument to his first mate. "Confirm their answer for me, Bilge."

Bilge took the glass and trained it on the brightly colored pennants flying on the *Jaguar*, flapping wildly in the high wind.

"I believe the response is ASSFUCK, cap'n."

Oz answered coolly, "Yes, I concur."

"What do you think it means, sir?"

"I believe, dear Bilge, it means that we are not to expect a reach-around."

Both men watched a flash and puff of gray smoke belch from one of the pirate ship's cannons, followed by a loud boom.

The thirty-two-pound iron ball screamed its fury as it closed the distance. Oz and Bilge watched it plow its way through the port side of the captain's quarters, tearing off a large chunk of the poop deck.

"Indeed" Oz said dispassionately, "right up the old alimentary canal."

The crew scrambled to bring the *LaSalle* about to firing position as the *Jaguar* hoisted sail.

Bilge shouted, "Return fire, sir?"

"No, we must close and board. Lady Ravenna is on that ship. We cannot ..."

Before the captain could finish his thought, a rippling of booms echoed, followed by the shriek of shells and the crash of impact to the *LaSalle's* port side midships. The boat lurched with the shock and men screamed in panic and agony from the decks below.

The pirate boat was now billowing sail and working its way to Oz's stern. He could see the men through the gun portals reloading.

"Give them a volley broadside!" the captain shouted.

Bilge relayed the order and bellowed at the helmsman to steer to port to escape encirclement by the fast-moving ship.

Thundering guns from below decks rattled the *LaSalle* and filled the air with powder smoke. Oz and Bilge grinned watching the shells tear through the pirate's main gun deck, tearing wood, steel, and flesh, taking out two of Knox's cannons.

The ships began circling each other like sharks closing on prey, faster in the growing wind, each new volley firing fewer shells as they disarmed their enemy's guns. Men still whole or slightly wounded on both boats struggled to pull starboard guns across the deck to rearm the port side, losing gun and man overboard when the ship listed and bucked in the rising waves like a mustang horse with an unwelcome rider.

The storm grew to full breath, sending the clouds above spinning in a wild, whirling funnel that pushed the ships ever faster and closer in their dance of death. Smoke-dark brume whirled in furious corkscrew and descended toward the axis of the fight, sweeping the waves into a swirling, churning whirlpool that deepened with every second.

The maelstrom grew, sucking the ships ever inward. The wind tore sails and shattered masts as the guns silenced, unable to raise their barrels to aim, so far did the boats lean in toward the inexorable vortex.

Sailors no longer cared to manage sail, wheel, or gun, desperately gripping whatever they could find to keep from washing overboard. But overboard they flew, their screams unheard over the roaring wind.

The funnel cloud mated with the whirling water and spawned a massive typhoon, the ships now without hope of escape, spinning in the merciless gyre.

Having lashed himself to the quarterdeck railing, Oz glared through the darkening mists at the *Jaguar*, swirling opposite the *LaSalle* into the same hellish undertow. There he spied the hated Knox, tied likewise to a mast, shaking his fist and screaming some futile oath swallowed in the deafening cyclone.

Bound next to him stood Ravenna, too frightened to scream, her tortuously splendid locks still gleaming and well managed despite the high humidity and merciless gale force winds.

Whether the ships would be sucked down into the water or up into the clouds neither man could discern, but with their last thought both knew death was their fate and hell their destination.

Chapter 9 - Cue the
Scholarly Simian Savior

Knox Bloodworthe's soul rose from the inky blackness of death-in-life and broke through the surface, but he did not open his eyes. The fires of hell burned his back while the roar of the ocean deafened his ears. Hell tasted like sand and seawater, which he expected, but he kept his eyes shut to avoid the sight of the demon that was stabbing his face with a pitchfork.

He finally peeked through slit eyelids, expecting to see a hideous creature personally assigned to drive him mad until the stars winked out in the heavens.

Behind the huge claw probing and pinching his face stood two tall, soulless eyes. The claw reached out and pinched his nose hard, making Knox yelp in pain and push himself up from the sand.

The crab, as startled as the captain, crouched and raised its claws in defense.

Touching his nose and finding blood there enraged Knox such that he raised his arm and hammered the opportunistic scavenger with his massive fist.

As the crushed crustacean twitched its last, the pirate turned over to sit in the sand and take in his surroundings.

The sea stretched out before him to the far horizon devoid of land or ship's mast. Sandy beach ran to his left and right for a quarter mile or more, curving away and disappearing into dense tropical greenery of broadleaved fern and palm trees. Behind, jungle growth seemed to thicken with every foot inland. Above, only cloudless sky and blazing sun.

Knox struggled to his feet, unsteady and still spitting grains of sand from his lips. Aware of powerful thirst for the first time, he surmised he was not dead in hell, but alive and standing on the coastline of a land he did not recognize and had not seen named on any map.

He stood and took stock of himself, bruised and cut here and there but nothing worse than the wound he'd received from the scuttling shellfish. His rapier was still in scabbard on his belt, along with a long dagger and a pistol, the latter useless unless he could find dry powder and shot. He took a kerchief from his coat pocket and tied it tightly over his head to keep from baking his brain in the relentless sun.

His body screaming for water, he scanned inland looking for signs of a direction to take.

A wave crested, rolled in with a roar to sweep over and past his boots, then receded with a prolonged sigh. In the quiet before the next wave, Knox heard voices, shouts and screams, somewhere down the beach past a small jetty of rocks.

Uncaring if they were friend or foe, only that they might have water, he set out down the beach at a labored, slow run.

His body ached and his lungs struggled for breath as he made the short distance, climbed the rocks and laid down at the crest to peer over.

Squid was struggling to pull Adelaide from the waves while she screeched curses and slapped at the old sailor with tired, soft blows.

Ravenna lay on the sand just above the water line, poised as if napping with her knees tilted together to her left side, right arm splayed and the other at her belly. Her hair, still insufferably shiny despite soaking in the ocean brine, surrounded her head like a golden halo. Eyes closed and lips pursed, she reminded Knox of a little girl dreaming of butterflies and zebras and moonbeams and fairy tales.

But, said the other voice in his head, the dead often look peaceful.

Knox lifted himself over the rocks and ran toward her, shouting at Squid and waving his arms.

Squid waved back and took a solid slap to the cheek for his trouble. He again pinned the struggling nun's arms and manhandled her the last few feet out of the water where he let her drop and fell himself, flopping over to his back and taking deep, raspy breaths.

Adelaide did the same, uttering a wheezy curse with every exhale.

Knox reached Ravenna, threw himself to his knees beside her and reached out to feel the pulse at her throat but stopped, wanting to let the beautiful girl keep dreaming, or the dead girl to reach heaven undisturbed.

Living or dead, she changed in the pirate's eyes for a moment, becoming what he'd never seen her as before, a beautiful and desirable woman. He watched her bosom rise and fall, taking relief in the sign of life. Her face lost the porcelain perfection of a doll and seethed with life. Her delicate and symmetrical features, no longer the artisanal mask of female comeliness, he saw as the face of a living, breathing woman with a heart and a brain and the youth and vigor to let both have their way in the world.

Then a sheer and unadorned lust to possess her beauty inflamed him. His own breath deepened, mind alive with thoughts of her that ignored his years of planning and his cunning maneuvers to trade her for gold. The gold laid out before him, here in the burning sand, he suddenly desired more than any coin or jewel.

She stirred, coughed weakly and turned her face away from the torturous sunlight toward where his shadow protected her.

She opened her eyes. "Am I dead?"

"No, good lady."

"So, you also are not dead?"

"No."

"Oh dear." She smiled weakly. "What a pity. I had so hoped to see you killed."

"Don't despair of that, Lady Ravenna. There's still time."

More voices from farther down the beach drew the pirate's attention. Three of his men were wading into the surf to retrieve flotsam from the ship, a few broken planks and a barrel.

"Squid!" he shouted, "Go help the men. I'll get the women into the shade and look for water."

"Aye, sir" the old salt gasped. He struggled to rise and limped toward his shipmates, shouting orders.

Knox stood and held out his hand. "Here, Lady, let's get you out of this sun."

"I can manage," she said, waving him off. "Go help Sister Adelaide. She's more in need than I."

"As you wish" he said, surprised at how easily he accepted her command.

Seeing the pirate approach her, Adelaide set off a fireworks show of curses.

"Touch me not, thou foul trunk of humours, thou bolting-hutch of beastliness! I would beat thee, but I would infect my hands, thou currish, obscene, greasy tallow-catch!"

Knox laughed. "I'll give your convent their due, sister. They certainly teach a colorful vocabulary."

She made no other attempt at resisting as he lifted her up and over his shoulder but continued her litany of maledictions.

"Thou goatish, doghearted pignut! Thou whoreson pox pustule!"

He carried the nun to where Ravenna waited and followed her lead into the jungle canopy.

Just a few yards walking brought them to a clearing cooled by dense shade. Knox set the now quiet Adelaide down gently and leaned her against a tree trunk. She kept her eyes closed and with a labored breath whispered, "Thou clotpole."

Ravenna kneeled by Adelaide and lifted one of her eyelids, then the other. The old woman's eyes were cloudy and bloodshot, and they rolled back as her consciousness wavered.

"She must have water soon" the lady said. "Go find some."

The pirate captain nodded and turned, then stopped. Before he could muse a moment on his sudden status as second-in-command, Ravenna said, "Well? Get on with it!"

He headed off into the thicket, shaking his head.

Knox relied on experience and his now burning thirst to aid his search. He scanned the ground for dampness and tested vines, cutting their stalks with his dagger to sample the sap. He followed an animal trail that might lead to a spring or pool while watching for birds overhead that could be flying to or from water.

He found nothing and grew weary, faint, and dizzy. He began to despair of making it back to the others when a sudden loud rustling in the high branches and a skittering animal call spun him around, dagger in one hand and his useless pistol in the other.

A small monkey, long haired and black with a white belly, leapt from one high branch to another closer to the ground. He peered at the pirate with bright, curious eyes. His cheeks were white and feathery, like the mutton-chop sideburns cultivated by vain old men. He gripped the branch where he sat with clawed feet and hands, his long tail curling and flexing like a curious snake.

Knox relaxed and smiled. "I'll wager you know where to find water, eh, little chimp?"

"As a matter of fact" the monkey said, "I do know where to find water, but if you persist in referring to me as a chimp I shall never reveal its whereabouts."

Knox stared for a stunned moment, searching for the part of his brain that could accept a talking chimp. Not finding it, he said, "What?"

"Oh dear, oh dear, we're not off to a stellar start, are we? Let's try again. As part of my previous utterance I said I know where to find water, yes?"

"Yes, but—"

"Tut, tut, do not interrupt. I then said that if you persist in referring to me as a chimp, I will not take you to water, yes?"

"Uh, are you talking, or have I gone mad with thirst?"

"Mad or no, you are a less than adequate student. Answer the question."

"Yes."

"So, from these two statements, what conclusion can you reach?"

"Conclusion?"

"Think. Your life and the lives of your friends hang in the balance."

Knox dropped his eyes to the ground, shook his head and tried to think. All that came to him was, *I've died after all, and this is some insane god's idea of hell.*

The monkey sighed and rolled its large, dark eyes. "I'll give you a hint." He curled his long tail upward and pointed to it.

Knox looked and said, "You have a tail."

"Your powers of observation are not impaired. Neither is your talent for stating the obvious. Do chimps have tails?"

"I don't know."

"Then you should not be referring to anyone as a chimp if you do not know what one looks like, should you?"

Knox gaped and could say nothing, deciding that a real hell with fire and pitchforks would be preferable to this nightmare.

Again the monkey sighed, folding his arms and stroking his feathery cheek. "Oh, this just won't do. You have blotted your copybook, sir. Apes don't have tails, and chimps are apes. In this taxonomy, there are monkeys, and there are apes. So, which am I?"

Wishing he had dry powder enough to put a pistol ball in his head, Knox said, "Monkey?"

"There now, not so difficult, eh?"

"Water." Knox was now reduced to the intellect of a clam.

"Right behind you."

He turned and found a bubbling spring in a rock outcropping that he swore was not there a moment before. It cascaded and happily burbled into a pool at the base. He fell to his knees and crawled, thrust his face into the clear pool and gulped mouthfuls of the cool, fresh water.

The monkey smiled. "Funny how one can find what one seeks if one simply applies one's logical faculties, eh, what?"

Knox lifted his head and sputtered, gaining back some of his sanity. "What are you called, monkey who talks and wields magic?"

"Many have called me... Tim."

"Many?"

"Oh yes, we get your sort here all the time. But they all die. You will as well."

Chapter 10 - Eat or Be Eaten

By the time the sun dimmed to orange and stood on the lip of the horizon, the day's heat had given way to a chilling ocean breeze.

Knox and his tiny crew made camp at the spring. They laid the planks on rocks to make benches and gathered enough dry wood for a small fire. Knox sent the three sailors in search of more wood and food. Lady Ravenna and Sister Adelaide sat warming themselves by the crackling flames while Knox pried the barrel open with his dagger.

All were delighted when he handed out apples from Packard, their first meal as a company of marooners.

Sitting between Adelaide and Ravenna, Squid attacked his apple with vigorous hunger, quickly finishing it off with great slurping bites and loud chewing, drawing spiteful glances from the nun as she nibbled hers.

"Must you devour that like a ravenous animal, varlet?" she chided.

The first mate masticated the last of the core, stem and all, and swallowed with difficulty. "Ah, but I am a ravenous animal, sister. An' once these give out, we'll all be such. At least the apples will keep us from the delicate question for a time."

Ravenna asked, "What delicate question?"

"Who eats and who's eaten."

Both women stared at Squid, bits of apple suspended in their frowning mouths.

"Custom o' the sea" said the old salt, smiling. "When we find ourselves staring into the grinning death's head of starvation, we draw lots and eat the loser."

Adelaide's gorge rose. She spit her bite of apple into the fire. "Thou liest, whey-faced bum boil."

Knox finished the last of his apple and threw the core in the fire. "No, sister, Squid is telling the truth. Terrible things happen at sea, you know."

"My husband was a sailor and he never told me of such abomination."

Ravenna swallowed a bite of apple and gasped. "You had a husband?"

"Er, well, yes. For a time."

"Only a short time" said Squid. "Ye likely killed him 'afore he had a chance to tell you about the Custom."

"You *killed* a husband?" Ravenna shook her head in disbelief.

"You killed a *husband*?" Knox repeated.

The nun shrugged her shoulders. "It was him or me."

Knox smiled at Ravenna. "I told you that a pirate lives within us all. The good sister is proof."

"I'm no pirate, dank dewberry. He was a right bastard who got his just deserts, not an innocent girl and her matron, like we whom you have most foully wronged."

Knox winked. "Everyone is a right bastard who gets their just deserts, pirate nun. Death comes to us all, whether at the end of a blade or in the down of a bed. Nobody gets out alive, the pious and chaste or the profane and promiscuous. In the end, all debts are paid and all accounts balanced."

Adelaide tossed the last of her uneaten apple into the fire and whispered, "Puking puttock."

Ravenna asked Squid, "So, what of this Custom of the Sea? Do you mean you become cannibals?"

"If it comes to that, aye. Everyone in the party draws lots, cap'n included, an' the loser is Sailor Stew. Every man who goes to sea learns the Custom."

Ravenna grinned, a tinge of evil pleasure around her eyes. "Have you ever tasted Sailor Stew then, Squid?"

"Ah, well, the first rule to Custom o' the Sea, is you don't talk 'bout Custom of the Sea. Right cap'n?"

Bloodworthe nodded and smiled. "Aye, that's true. Otherwise we'd end up reminiscing around the fire about how old Bixby went well with a hearty red wine and Farnsworth made for a savory chilled salad."

Ravenna laughed a little too happily and held her hand over her smiling lips when Adelaide scowled at her.

"Well" said the nun, pointing to Squid, "I'd certainly never eat you, rank lewdster. Your meat is foul rotten, like your soul is black and condemned, thou weedy, toad-spotted scut."

"I'd eat *you*, sweet Sister Adelaide, in that way or any other you'd care to try."

The old mate shook with restrained laughter, grinning at Adelaide and nudging her with his elbow, until she suddenly jammed her thumb into one eye. He fell over and landed on his back, holding his face and laughing between grunts and groans of pain.

Ravenna laughed quietly, then cleared her throat and forced her lips downward when Adelaide again glanced at her with matronly scorn.

"So," she said to Knox, "what else did you find in your scouting besides a magic, talking monkey?"

"Well, as I told you, Tim said that this is an island, and not big. I climbed a hill high enough to see half of it, so I believe him. I'll start sending the men in pairs east and west tomorrow, looking for provisions and to map what they find. But especially, to learn if Oz made it here as well. If so, I will track him down and kill him with pain."

Ravenna gasped and glared at Knox. "If you find Oz or any of his men, then you must join forces to get us off this island and home to Hudson."

"I'll do no such thing."

"We've no hope of survival if you insist on pursuing your useless vendetta!"

The pirate turned an angry eye at the lady. "Useless?"

"Yes, useless. If you kill Oz, but cannot escape this island, what use is it?"

"An eternity in hell will be good enough for me if I watch that bastard die on my blade."

"You will do everything possible to get me home, including to work with any man we can find!"

Knox matched the blaze in the blond woman's deep blue eyes. "Who do you think you are ordering about, girl? I'm the captain here, and I decide our every step, not you!

"I am Lady Ravenna of Hudson, and you will return me to my father in exchange for your ransom. I will then wed Captain Oz, and he will destroy you and any who follow you."

Knox shouted, "I told you that Oz must die, and if the gods of the sea did not take him, then I must do it myself. Everything else comes second! Including you, you ... technical virgin!"

Squid sat on his knees, elbows on the plank next to Adelaide, holding his wounded eye and gaping at the drama before him.

Adelaide likewise watched in awe of this strange turn of events.

Ravenna's face turned mocking and haughty. "A virgin who the bloodthirsty, murdering, rapacious Knox Bloodworthe won't even rape. I'm more to be feared than the Scourge of the Seaways!"

"Gods of the deep" whispered the old sailor.

"Salacious preserve us" whispered the old nun.

Knox drew his dagger and bellowed, "If you stand between me and my vengeance, I shall slit your throat where you stand, and we'll have virgin for supper instead of sailor!"

A man's scream, blood-curdling with terror and pain, tore the fabric of the air and shocked the jungle to stillness. The four people around the campfire froze and stared into the lush green beyond the clearing.

A second scream from the doomed man was cut short as he gurgled his last breath. Then shouts of more men followed and grew louder. Two of Knox's crew burst through the thicket into the little campsite clearing, screaming and babbling. The first ran on into the jungle on the far side. Knox grabbed the second and wrestled the panicked, shrieking sailor to the ground.

He held him down by the shoulders, shaking him to wake from his nightmare. "What happened, man? What are you running from?"

"M-m-monster!"

"Monster? What, an animal? A beast?"

Squid stood and drew his short cutlass, watching the path where the men had come.

"Monster! A-a-lizard! Walking like a man, two men tall! Great scales down the back, eyes like the fires of hell!"

"Come to your senses, dog! How can a lizard—"

The captain's question was answered by a great screeching roar, like a beast whelped from the unholy union between a lion and an eagle.

Squid breathed, "What in the name of the sea gods...?"

Adelaide held her hands to her breast and pleaded for protection from any saint who would listen.

Ravenna gasped, "What could it be?"

"Well, ladies and gentlemen" came a voice with perfect diction and a cultured accent, "that, you should know, is Kalakuta."

Tim the erudite monkey sat on a nearby branch, casually picking at a fingernail.

"Kala-whoo-a?" stuttered Squid.

"Kalakuta" Tim replied. "Repeat after me, class. Kal-Ah-Koo-Tah."

"Kal-Ah-Koo-Tah" the four lucid people echoed.

"Excellent. You are catching on well."

Seeing a talking monkey after watching his friend killed and half consumed by a twelve-foot, bipedal lizard monster, the fifth man promptly fainted.

"And who in blazes is Kalakuta?" Knox demanded.

"The god of this island" Tim answered.

"God?"

"Well, more a demigod, truth be told. A lesser deity, in the hierarchy of such beings. A minor god, perhaps third string. But a mean-tempered one, and in charge here, and hungry."

"Hungry?" asked wide-eyed Adelaide.

"Ravenous" answered the bored monkey.

"Can we defeat him?" asked the Lady of Hudson.

"Hmm. Well, the short answer is maybe."

"What's the long answer then?" demanded the pirate captain.

"The long answer is ... probably not."

Chapter 11 - Tea, Biscuits, and Monkey Poo

Some distance away, startled by the faint sound of a man killed and eaten by a twelve-foot, bipedal lizard monster, Captain Oz set his teacup in the saucer with a bit too much force. The delicate China clinked, and a small chip fell into the sand of the jungle clearing.

"I say, what in blazes was that?"

Bilge set another bit of driftwood on the small fire he'd built. "A man dyin', to be sure."

"One of ours?"

"Can't say from such a distance, sir."

"Hmm. No, of course not."

Oz took another sip from the delicate china cup and grinned his pleasure. "It was right resourceful of you to save my emergency chest from the *LaSalle*, dear Bilge. A cask of water, a bit of tea, some biscuits and sundries, and you have spared us the urgent but tedious task of scrabbling for survival."

"Among the sundries, captain, I managed to stow a bar of your favorite soap."

"Good man. I am too tired now, but in the morning I shall wash the stink of the sea from my body and clothes. I am, as always dear Bilge, in your debt."

The mate smiled. "Think nothin' of it, sir, my duty and naught more."

"You are too modest. You will be rewarded handsomely upon our return home."

A shriek of laughter from high in the trees shocked Oz into chipping the cup again. Bilge stood and drew his dagger. The high-pitched hilarity continued until the laugher was out of breath.

After a chuckling inhale, a high-pitched voice shouted, "Oh, fuck me! Ha ha! Return home? You stupid shitheads are gonna be breakfast for Kalakuta by dawn. Ha ha!"

Oz stood and shouted into the branches, "Who's there? Show yourself!"

"Eat shit, cock knocker!"

"Insult my captain, will you?" Bilge growled, "Come down and I'll slit your throat. We'll see how hard you laugh then!"

A high branch rustled, then a lower bent under some weight, sending a flock of nesting birds to take wing, a squawking cloud rising against the deepening red sky.

With a screech, a monkey suddenly dropped and landed on a low branch nearest Bilge. Its coat was black except for a white belly and feathery cheeks. The branch dipped under the weight and the primate waved its long tail to balance.

It fixed large, dark eyes on Bilge and shrieked, "Laugh this off, fat fuck!" Reaching behind, it filled its right hand with a gooey load of feces and pitched it at Bilge's face.

Only a quick duck saved the first mate from the worst of it. Rising, he wiped a small glob from his shoulder and scowled at the creature.

"I'll butcher you for dinner" Bilge swore, "then sew your wretched hide into a hat."

"You already wear your ass for a hat, you hairless, pink ape!"

The captain raised his hand. "Begging your pardon, but who might you be, foul-mouthed simian?"

The monkey turned its wide eyes to Oz and mocked, "Oh, begging your *parhhdon* is it? Oh my, aren't we *highborn*. *Parhhdon* me, *mater*, but I'm off to play the *grahhnd piahhno!*"

"Look here my good... monkey, there is no reason to be rude—"

"Oh, look here, *pater*, I'm off to the *cluhhb* for a round of tennis and tea with *Bahhbra* and *Biff*."

Oz huffed, "Enough of this" and handed his cup and saucer to Bilge. He bent down and took up a small rock as the monkey continued mocking, "Oh, pish and tosh, no more buttered *scohhnes* for me, *mater*, I'm off to meet *Eaton* and *Madeline* on the *crohhquet* lawn."

With a sweep of his arm Oz sent the rock flying straight into the monkey's forehead.

"Fuck!" the monkey cursed as he fell to the jungle floor with a thud and a groan.

Bilge smiled. "Fine throw, cap'n."

"Top rated bowler for the Packard Polecats, three years running."

"Brilliant, sir."

The two men ran to the unconscious monkey, Bilge with his dagger at the ready.

"May I kill him sir?"

"No, he may prove valuable."

"He'd be valuable in a good stew."

The monkey began rousing and groaned.

"No, I mean we may need his advice. He's obviously intelligent and knows this place."

"But he flung poo at me, cap'n."

"Consider it a wound in the line of duty, first mate."

Bilge frowned. "Aye, sir."

"Assholes" groaned the half-conscious monkey. "You didn't have to do that. I was just fuckin' with ya."

"Then cooperate," Oz said, wagging a finger, "or I will let Bilge here make you into a hat."

"Bilge, huh?" The monkey sat up and tenderly touched the lump growing on his skull. "That figures."

"I am Captain Ozymandias Wembleye."

The monkey grinned. "That figures, too."

"And you are?"

"Tom."

"Tom. Just Tom? Not Thomas, or —"

"Fuck off with that Thomas shit! What do I look like? Some posh toff like you, Ozzy-fucking-man-dee-ass?"

"Bilge?"

"I've got a few spices in the chest, sir. He'd go good wrapped in palm leaves and roasted."

"All right, dammit, don't get your digestive juices flowing. I'll be good."

Oz waved Bilge off. "Then be a good magical talking monkey and tell us where we are."

"The Island of Kalakuta."

Bilge said, "He mentioned that name, cap'n. Claimed we'd be Kalakuta's breakfast."

"So he did. Who is this Kalakuta, Tom?"

"He's in charge here."

"In charge? Like a governor, or— "

"Like a god."

Bilge asked, "What sort of god?"

Tom scoffed a laugh. "What sort do you think, bilge water? The nasty, mindless kind that fucks and kills and eats whatever and whoever it wants, not necessarily in that order."

Oz looked off toward the west. "Was that Kalakuta we heard earlier? That terrible, shrieking roar?"

"Yeah, that's him all right. Every time I hear that, I shit my pants. Or I would if I had pants."

Bilge said, "Then that was him, sir, killing a man."

"And eating him," said Tom, "or fucking him. Or both."

"And how does one go about defeating this Kalakuta?" asked the captain.

"Shit, man, do you always talk like that?" Tom went back to his mocking tone. "Oh, *pater*, how *does* one defeat a twelve-foot, ravenous, horny lizard-monster with big, nasty, pointy teeth? Shall we ask *Eaton* and *Madeline* while we play *crohhquet* and nibble on *cucuhhmbah* sandwiches?"

Bilge?

"Right sir, one monkey hat coming up."

Tom leapt to his feet and backed away, "No, no!, dammit. I'll help you, but it won't do any good."

"No?" asked Oz, "why not?"

"Because *one* does not defeat Kalakuta. You'll need a small army. And even then, chances are slim to none."

Captain Oz turned his gaze to the last of the burning red sun surrendering the horizon, his strategic mind working at full steam. "There may be more men where the dead one came from. We shall look for them tomorrow, Bilge."

"Aye cap'n."

Oz turned back to Tom. "What are his weaknesses, this god?"

Tom laughed. "Kalakuta ain't got no weaknesses, *pater*."

"Everyone, and everything, has a weakness, Thomas."

"Hey! Fuck you!"

Oz smiled. "Would you like a biscuit, Tom?"

"Biscuit?" Tom suddenly smiled, a greedy look to his eye. "Are they the shitty sailor kind, all hard and tasteless?"

"Yes."

Tom clapped his hands, his eyes bright. "Oh yes, I love those! Gimmee!"

The captain wagged a finger. "Manners?"

Tom frowned and sighed. "Okay, dammit. Please, *pater*, may I have a biscuit?"

"Yes, you may."

As they made their way to the sea chest, Tom muttered, "Thanks, asshole."

Chapter 12 - A Warning Ignored

Dawn broke over the island, rousing the animals and birds to frantic squawking and chirping before the sun ever peeked over the horizon of the azure sea.

While Bilge set about foraging for wood and food, Oz followed Tom's lead to where the foul-mouthed simian said he could bathe. Favorite soap in hand and towel over his shoulder, he left his blue captain's coat behind and walked through the brightening forest as Tom leapt from branch to branch just ahead.

"This lagoon, Tom. Is it far?"

"Naw, not far. We'd get there faster if you could follow me through the trees, instead of plodding along like some two-legged tortoise."

"I'm walking as fast as I can. In any case, I walk proudly upright as a man should."

"Heh, proud of moving slow and leaving your belly open to attack, are you? Your kind are a movable feast for the likes of Kalakuta."

"My kind are the masters of all creation, made in the image of God."

Tom laughed. "If that's true then God is a slow, stupid bag of guts that Kalakuta can catch, fuck and eat without breaking a sweat."

Oz glowered at the chattering monkey. "I have my sword. I can defend myself."

"Ho, you think so, do you? The Green Godlet will use that pig sticker of yours for a toothpick to clean your sinews outta his molars, shitass."

"That's quite enough out of you, Thomas. Let us continue our journey in silence."

"Oh right-o, *pater*. Let us *cohn-tin-ee-you* our journey, as it's such a *smahshing* day for a *strohll* about the *garhden*, what, what?"

The captain ignored the taunts and laughter until the monkey grew bored and silent.

The rising sun sent shafts of golden light through the canopy. Oz admired the beauty of the lush jungle, alive with brightly colored flowers and plants the likes of which he'd never seen. The loveliness led his thoughts to Ravenna, and to wonder if he'd ever see her again. Did she survive, and if so, would she be changed? Would she no longer desire him as her husband? She might very well despise him for failing to save her, leaving her stranded in this unknown, dangerous place.

Even if she does still want me, what would become of us? Is it any life for a woman of her breeding to live hand-to-mouth in this wild jungle, under constant threat of being killed and eaten, like prey?

Lost in reverie and rumination, Oz did not hear the roar of falling water growing louder. Tom startled him by dropping from the tree to the trail and announcing, "Here ya go, *pater*, Kalakuta Falls Lagoon."

Oz followed Tom through an arch of palms into a broad glade of open sand where a towering fifty-foot waterfall plunged like a bride's veil from a high, rocky cliff. It fed a deep pool with a broad, flat, rocky table in the center. The pool emptied into a fast-running stream that led off into the jungle toward the sea. The spray from the falls filled the air with the clean scent of cool refreshment and refracted the bright morning sunlight into a rainbow arc framing the cliff.

He gaped at the beauty of it all. "This wondrous place is named after Kalakuta?"

"*Everything* on this island is named after Kalakuta, *pater*."

"Yes, of course. Thank you for bringing me here, Tom."

"Live ta serve ya, fancy-pants. Listen, I'm off to scare up some breakfast. You enjoy your little spa trip, but a word of warning ..."

"Yes?"

"If you hear singing, ignore it. Don't go looking for who's doing the singing."

Oz frowned at Tom. "Indeed? Why so?"

"Just ... don't." The monkey leapt onto the nearest branch and disappeared into the canopy.

Confused but not concerned, Oz stripped down and stepped into the pool. The bracing, icy water made him gasp, but soon he warmed up and began scrubbing with his favorite soap and happily singing his boyhood song.

Rum-te-piddly, piddly rum,
Thrum the iddly-diddily drum.

He held his breath as he soaped his face and dunked himself to rinse. When he surfaced, he heard an eerie sound slowly rising and dropping in pitch, creating a strange and alluring melody. He turned toward the source and nearly fainted, the blood draining from his head, his heart fluttering in shock.

Being a lifelong sailor, he'd heard stories of mermaids, dismissing them as the lust-maddened fantasies of lonely men. But there, lounging on the flat rock at the center of the pool, sat a woman with long red hair falling in wavy tendrils over her taut, bare breasts, skin pale as alabaster, but with the long, light gray body of a dolphin where her legs should be, ending in a fluked tail. She lazily swung the tail back and forth as she toyed with her hair and, beaming a smile at Oz, sang her siren song.

"Ooo-eee-ooo-aah-ahh" she sang, her voice reaching the captain's ears and speeding directly to his heart, restoring its rhythm to a slow, strong beat. Another chorus of "Ooo-eee-ooo-aah-ahh" carried the vibrations lower into his belly, and farther still, reaching his loins and encircling there the very root of his sex.

He remembered Tom's warning and ignored it.

"Hello" he said.

"Hellooo" sang the mermaid.

"I am Captain Ozymandias Wembleye, but you may call me Oz."

"Ozzz" she sibilated and smiled, making the captain's skin tingle and his heart flutter.

"What may I call you?"

She said, "My name is," then drew a deep breath and screeched, "EEE-VEE-AROOO-VEE!," followed by a loud raspberry and a whistle in a rising pitch so resounding Oz covered his ears with his hands. She finished with a low, rumbling bellow, "Oooooooh!," then slapped her tail on the rock three times.

"I see" the captain said, slowly freeing his ears. "That's rather difficult for me to pronounce. May I call you Eve?"

"Oh, yes" she whispered, then suddenly dropped from the rock into the water.

She broke the surface facing Oz and before he could react embraced him and delivered a deep kiss, her tongue alive within his mouth, tasting faintly of the sea.

When she broke it off, still holding him tightly in her strong arms, he stammered, "What ... what was that for?"

"You've come to save us" she said and kissed him again.

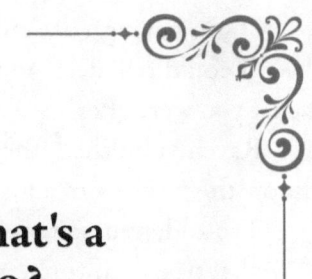

Chapter 13 - What's a Girl Gotta Do?

Ravenna lay in the grass beneath a great oak tree, languidly accepting the embrace and caresses of two men, one fondling her breasts while the other lightly stroked her labia as they took turns kissing her lips, cheeks, and neck. She could never quite make out their faces but sensed their smiles and their warm breath on her as their hands kindled flames of desire within her belly.

She reached out and filled each hand with a hard cock, stroking both and feeling them pulse and grow under her fingers. She whispered, "Please" and guided one to her sex and the other toward her mouth. The men rose to the task, one moving between her legs while the other hovered over her head. She was about to take both inside her when an ear-piercing screech from a large bird blew it all away — the men and the tree and the grass and the fiery longing in her loins — like smoke in a windstorm.

Half awake, she found it wasn't a bird screeching, but Adelaide struggling to free her wrists from Ravenna's tight grasp and yelling, "Wake up girl! Wake up!"

Being stronger than the old woman, she had nearly managed to pleasure herself with one set of fingers and suck the others before awareness made her release the nun, sit up and cry, "I am so sorry, dear sister!"

Adelaide rubbed her reddened wrists and said, "No harm done, child."

"I was having a dream ... a wonderful dream."

"I could tell, dear, and no need to recall it for me. I know full well what you were after."

Ravenna blushed, then welled tears and cried, "I fear I shall never know the pleasure of a man's touch, Adelaide."

The old nun softened her smile and patted the lady's shoulder. "Well, if true then you'll never know the pain of a man's touch either or suffer the loss of a touch you loved so well."

"I'd rather have the pain so as to know the pleasure."

"Aye, and there's the pity of it. Can't have one without the other."

Adelaide pulled Ravenna close and let the girl cry on her shoulder for a while.

When she calmed, Ravenna looked around the tiny encampment, her still unbelievably shiny, flaxen locks casting off golden sparks of morning sunlight. "Where are the men?"

"Squid is leading the sailors on a hunt. Knox said he was off in search of Captain Oz."

"Oh no!" The lady's eyes widened, and she put her delicate hand over her gaping lips. "Oh, I mustn't let him. If he finds Oz he will kill him!"

"Surely Oz can defend himself, dear."

"No, this is terrible. Knox told me the reason for his blood vendetta, and he will have the advantage of a terrible rage. I saw it in his eyes." She stood and turned her head every direction. "Which way?"

Adelaide rose unsteadily and grasped at Ravenna's arm. "You'll not follow."

"I will! Tell me which way."

"And leave me here, alone?"

Ravenna gazed into her matron's eyes, her own tearing up and pleading. "Please, give me your permission."

Adelaide saw the desperation on Ravenna's face. "Aye. You must go." She pointed westward.

Ravenna embraced Adelaide and kissed her withered cheek. "Bless you sister."

She ran into the jungle, heedless of danger as she made her way through the dense trees and vines and scanned the ground for the captain's boot prints.

Soon she was dizzy from running and the fear gripping her heart. She struggled to call out, "Captain! Captain!," but her breath was shallow and her cries weak. Her footfalls were loud and her struggle through the dense foliage made great crashing noises that were sure to attract the attention of predators. The panic rose and she cried out in gasps until something incredibly strong captured her, gripped her about the arms and body and tackled her to the ground.

She started to scream, but a massive dark-skinned hand clamped over her mouth. A man's gruff voice hissed "Shhh!" into her ear. She still struggled until Knox whispered, "Be still, girl! You'll get us killed! It's me!"

When she gave up her fight, Knox loosened his grip and slowly took his hand away. "It's me" he said again, softly, his breath warm against her ear.

The fire of panic that had coursed through her veins transformed through an alchemy of the blood, turning the sting of fear into a deep warmth of safety infusing her sinews. Still fighting for breath, she felt his body close against her back, his embrace still tight, pressing against her breasts. The pain of the hard touch shifted from discomfort to a welcome ache of longing. The pace of her breathing slowed but deepened, her inhale drinking in his strong musk that tantalized her nose and rushed on to her heart, fanning the flames of her desire.

She heard his breath quicken and felt it hot on her neck. Taking his massive, callused hand in her delicate fingers, she pulled it back to her mouth and kissed the palm with soft, trembling lips, then arched her back to press her hips against him.

For a moment, Knox pushed back, and she felt his flesh rise against her. Guiding his hand to her breast and turning her face to him drew a tortured, shuddering sigh from deep in his chest. She shifted so his now hard pillar found the cleft of her buttock and pushed back again, making him answer the rhythm with another of his own pelvic echoes.

Rolling to face him, Ravenna clutched his cock through his trousers, gasped at the length and width beneath her hand and whispered, her voice more growl than human word, "Please."

He answered with a deep, hard kiss, his teeth clattering against hers, his tongue plunging, his rumbling, animal groan vibrating their lips. This fueled her fire so that she jerked at his rod and spread her legs, trying to pull him into her.

He knelt over her, eyes flickering like a fire dancing to the breath of a panting bellows, his mouth half smile and half baring of fangs. She tugged at his pants, his belt, again moaning, "Please, please!"

The blaze in his countenance never flagged, but changed, like a wind blowing a campfire to a new compass point. His eyes wide, still laboring to breathe, he rose up, then staggered back to stand and lean against a nearby tree.

She lay before him hiking her long silk skirts high to expose herself to him, the pale skin of her legs speckled pink with the flush of her lust, the petals of her flower wide and wet, taking her breath in gulps and between each gasp sighing a plaintive, breathless, "Please."

He drank in her beauty and her rutting enchantment, his hand at his heart, and said, "No."

Ravenna cried, a disconsolate wail starting quiet, weak, and growing until she shrieked so loud a flock of birds in the trees took flight with a loud susurration of wing beats. The small, scurrying animals of the jungle went silent.

Knox hung his head, closed his eyes, and quietly wept.

Sometime later, he whispered, "You will be glad we did not when this is all over."

The lady's laughter startled the pirate. She began giggling, her mirth rising as her desire had before, until she laughed open-throated and full-winded, releasing the tension and ache that lust and grief had implanted in her body.

She collected herself, closing her legs and smoothing her gown, then chuckled, "You think so, do you?"

"Yes. When I collect your ransom and take you home, your honor will be intact, and you will find a new husband, one worthy of you, your station and your... undeniable beauty and allure."

Again she laughed. "Undeniable? You denied me."

"Yes. But I am a pirate, hard of heart and evil of spirit. And I have a plan for you that will free me from pirating for the rest of my days. You are... you are only a means to an end."

"Oh" she breathed, "you lying bastard."

"What?"

"You know full well that we may never escape this island. This is our world now, for as long as we can manage to live. You lie to yourself."

New sparks flickered in his eyes. "I will not tolerate—"

"You lie to me, saying I'm chattel, saying you are hard of heart. I felt you now, touching me, kissing me with the thirst of a man withering all these years without love. I felt your hunger, your need, and when I opened to you there was no doubt but that you wanted and needed me. *Me*!"

Ravenna stood and dusted her clothes. "But I see your lies are more powerful than your lust, or your love! You will persist in your madness, and I will die here with nothing, not even your touch, all to satisfy a ghost, the ghost of your long dead Bonnie. You trade life, living flesh, for death, for dry bones!"

The pirate's face now creased into a grimace of embarrassed anger. He pointed at her, shouting, "Woman, you will not speak of her ever again! You profane her memory with your words. And I will find a way to escape this hellish place and return you for my ransom, glad to be rid of you!"

"Liar!" the lady screamed. "You said you are a better man than Oz, but you're not! You are not half what he is, strong, brave, and honest!"

"Honest! That murderer? That ambusher, honest?"

"He gave you and your ilk what you deserved! He will be truthful to me if he still lives. But you will not, and I've offered my everything to a man who can give nothing!"

Ravenna sobbed her last words and sped off through the thicket in the direction of the camp.

Knox stood as if rooted to the ground. Stricken by her words, her truth, her beauty and the last effervescence of desire in his veins, he could not follow her.

To restore a tiny bit of pride, he shouted, "Go back to the camp and stay there! If I find Oz, you will not want to see his end!"

Ravenna ran on, fighting to stop her tears, her mind ablaze with anger and confusion, her heart aching with the pang of loss, her loins still hot with ardor.

Approaching the camp, she heard the men there talking and laughing as they dressed out some animal they'd killed. She stopped running and moved quietly around the camp, skirting it wide to avoid notice. Once on the far side and out of earshot, she quickened her pace. Knox had not found Oz traveling west from their camp. She would search eastward, toward the sun now lifting to mid-morning, and if she found him, she would have at last what she craved more than her next breath — a man to love who loved her, who would be true to her, and who would give her the snarling, animalistic, fluid-drenched shagging she so desperately desired.

"God, or Devil if it comes to that" she panted as she ran, "let me find him and you may take my soul for payment, for it will no longer be my own."

Chapter 14 - The Garden of Cetaceous Delight

Still held tightly in the mermaid's grip, Oz reluctantly surrendered her tongue and broke off the kiss. His heart beat fast and strong, and his body crackled with desire, feeling her warm breasts held tight to his chest, her slippery, writhing body pressed to his and making his cock stand grow with every breath.

"Rescue us?" he sputtered, "Rescue who? From what?"

"My people, the Merfolk of this island. We are prisoners of Kalakuta, and he is killing us off."

"I was told he's the god of this island."

She shook her head. "Only because he is so powerful, no one can defeat him. He arrived some twenty years ago and began devouring us. We lived here in peace for a thousand years before he came. He kills and eats at least one of us each day, and our numbers are dwindling fast."

Hearing this changed the heat in Oz's body, his lust cooling and his anger warming. "Have you tried to kill him?"

"We have tried, but his magic is stronger than ours. And since we cannot fight him on land, we are helpless. He can scoop one of us from the water with one hand, devouring his catch swiftly and terribly, making the victim suffer as much as possible before death. And he... he sometimes defiles the poor soul before eating them alive."

"The monster" Oz whispered.

Eve's face lit into a beaming smile. "But now, you are here, dear Oz, to rescue me and my people."

"You keep saying your people."

"Yes, I am Queen of the Merfolk. They are my subjects, my people. All the sadder that makes me since I cannot save them." The Mer Queen's bright smile dimmed, and her eyelids dropped in shame. "We will be made extinct if Kalakuta is not defeated."

"But, if you cannot defeat him with magic, what am I to do?"

Her face brightened again, her eyes wide and shimmering with hope. "Legends tell of a magic talisman hidden in a cave somewhere on the island. This talisman, a totem pillar of rare stone, is said to have the power to destroy the beast. A wizard guards the cave and the talisman who challenges seekers with a puzzle. Solve the puzzle, and the talisman is yours."

"Where is this cave?"

"None of us know. We can't travel over land to find it. That's why you are here!"

The queen again pressed herself to Oz's body and brought her lips close to his. "Whatever good fortune we have left has sent you to find the talisman and kill Kalakuta. You must, please, dear Captain Oz!"

Her sweet breath, hot against his lips, again changed where the fire in his body kindled. Her hands moved down his back toward his haunches, pulling him harder against her, inflaming his own magic totem pillar.

Again she whispered, "Please."

He found himself struggling for breath. "I... I will do everything in my power, Queen Eve, to defeat Kalakuta and release the Merfolk from his deadly reign. You have my word as an officer."

Her eyes now glistened with a deep radiance. "My hero. Do this, and I will be yours entirely, forever. You will be made King of the Merfolk, and I will be your queen, and we will live in bliss for the rest of our days."

Again, Oz stammered, "I... well, you see, I..."

She firmly gripped his buttock with one hand while the other slipped between them and took hold of his now fully erect member. "Let us" she whispered, "consummate our love here and now, to seal my promise to you of undying love and loyalty."

The stroking scrambled the captain's sense. Up, down, up again, the familiar grip and rhythm lulled him into reverie. He started to whisper his bath time tune, "*Rum-te-piddly, piddly-rum.*"

"Take me, my king."

The words helped waken him to the moment. "But surely you don't... I mean, the drawings I've seen show no... you aren't, er, shall we say, equipped with the necessary? For, for..."

Her smile grew hot under heavily lidded eyes. Still grinding his stalk, with her other hand she guided his fingers to the slit on the underside of her dolphin body. It opened easily to the press of his fingers, and she guided him within.

"But I am" she purred, "equipped. As you can tell."

"Oh, my" Oz mouthed without breath. Then, at an insistent yank on his vibrating manroot, he squeaked, "Oh, my!"

She leaned back in the water and pulled him onto her, guiding him to the target. "Ride me, my king" she cried, "let us become one!"

He did as she asked, his weight shifting forward and sending his cock plunging within her slit.

She held him there, floating a moment, her mouth agape and her eyes closed, moaning a low, crooning sound, "oouuuooouuuu!" as her tail undulated slowly in the water.

Oz's breath stopped. His heart fluttered. The sensation caused by the sheer envelopment of his turgid stalk was unlike anything Bilge had ever given him. Fully ensconced from root to tip, her slow, rhythmic motions squeezed and released him with an agonizingly delicious milking action. He groaned quietly, unable to form words or coherent thoughts, his eyes drinking in the incandescent loveliness of her face, her eyes, her hair, her red-lipped mouth, the unadulterated pleasure she was taking from their copulation.

Then her eyes burned into his, her smile turned womanly wicked, and she said, "Hold on, my king."

Slowly at first, she pumped her tail in the water, swimming backward with Oz riding. He tightened his hug around her waist, clasped her with his legs as if astride a horse, and let the deeper, wider thrust of her pelvis work him within her. She swam around the rock once at an easy pace, now beginning to gasp and giggle with delight, as Oz felt himself pulled deeper within her with every thrust. She rose and fell in the water, and he with her, his cock growing harder and more sensitive than he ever thought possible, his balls aching with anticipation of release.

Suddenly, she gripped him by both cheeks and shouted, "Take my breath, my love!" She covered his mouth in a tight kiss. Before he could do anything, understand anything, she dove under the water and flailed her fluked tail wildly, rushing them along at high speed.

Again she circled the rock, her powerful tail propelling them faster, the thrashing making Oz's engorged stalk pound within her, drawing him closer to orgasm with every movement. He tried to hold his breath, fearing he would drown, but gave out an agonized gasp and drew a frightened inhale. He found he could breathe, Eve sharing her air with him, and as they sped along, circling the rock again and again, their respiration joined in rhythm and pace as they grunted and groaned their shared pleasure.

Faster she swam them, and deeper into the pool, but Oz did not lack for air. He surrendered himself to the impossible moment, the unendurable pleasure, no longer caring if he lived or died, only that this inexorable joy of body and heart should go on forever.

Then, as they sank deeper and swam faster, he felt himself rising to the verge of eruption. Eve shuddered under him, her guttural cries in his mouth and throat growing as ragged as his. His balls drew up and his taint tightened in the last moments before the point of no return. The slick, hot, welcoming home of her sex shuddered with her own climax as he felt the first welcome ache of release.

When the moment arrived, Eve suddenly swept her tail to turn them upward, and with a few powerful strokes of her fluke, broke the surface and sent them skyward. Before they reached apogee they broke their kiss and screamed their delight as Oz's cock pumped flood after flood of man seed into her, and her fishy flesh quivered and pulsed to receive it. Still in the throes, Eve expertly inverted them with a twist of her strong body, so that when gravity pulled them down, they entered the water headfirst, a last flap of her tail sounding a loud, mighty splash.

No longer swimming, the lovers sank in the water holding each other tight, their kiss now tender and sweet. They quieted, and floated upward, breaking the surface gently as the last throbs of pleasure spread through their blood like the echoes of thunder after a storm has passed.

How long he rested on her strong, sleek body floating peacefully he could not tell. His cheek lay on her breasts, his lips softly kissing her nipple or tasting the tang of the sea in the tendrils of her luxurious hair.

She cooed a lullaby and stroked his cheek, smiling and kissing his forehead.

He finally stirred, lifted his head to look into her eyes, and gave her a chaste kiss with gentle lips. "I love you, dear Eve. I am yours forever."

"My beloved" she answered, "I always knew you would arrive."

She moved them toward the edge of the lagoon and helped Oz as he reluctantly dismounted. They held each other for a time, before she parted them and, with sad eyes, moved away.

"I know you will be victorious" she said as she swam toward the waterfall. "I know you will save us, and me, and we will live as merfolk for all our days."

"I will not fail you, darling Eve."

With that, she swam through the veil of the falls, and was gone.

He watched the ripples where she submerged slowly fade away, smiling, his body alive with a delight and mysterious lightness he'd never known.

A sound, then another, pulled him from his reverie. Somewhere beyond the clearing to the west, he heard some animal crashing through the underbrush, and the sound of running feet.

Now alert to danger, Oz pulled himself from the lagoon and ran to where his clothes lay carefully folded on a nearby rock. He threw his long, white shirt over his head, pulled it down to his thighs and drew his rapier from its scabbard, bracing himself for the onslaught of he knew not what.

Then a cry, high pitched and desperate, sounding from somewhere still beyond the tree line.

"Oz! My dear Oz! Where are you?"

His eyes bulging, he whispered, "Ravenna?"

Chapter 15 - Mind if I Cut In?

As Ravenna's calls grew louder and closer, two sides of Oz argued in the recesses of his skull.

Run and hide! said the one.

Answer her, fool! chided the other.

The soul-changing events of the past hour froze the captain with indecision, his twin minds bickering like hagglers in a market, arguing over Ravenna and Eve like they were rare jewels. Incapable of decisive action, Fate made the choice for him.

Ravenna burst through the foliage at the edge of the sandy lagoon and stopped, staring at the captain with unbelieving eyes. Her long, golden hair was disturbingly clean, groomed, and beauteous, despite all that she had suffered in a day and a night, her arduous journey through the jungle, and her lack of bathing. She panted as she stared, her face shifting from disbelief to recognition to joy in three heartbeats.

The lady squealed an unintelligible string of jubilant syllables as she sprinted toward Oz with outstretched arms.

Oz dropped his sword and caught her, the force of her embrace nearly toppling him. She babbled and wept and kissed his lips, cheeks, and neck, her face flushed red and wet with tears. He returned her kisses chastely, avoiding any chance of a prolonged, passionate osculation, and cooed to calm her. When she pressed her head against his chest and cried her last, he held her tight and ran his hand through her hair, examining the tendrils and wondering what conditioning creme she used that had so well protected the annoyingly lovely locks from sun, sea, and sand.

"Oh, Oz!" she cried into his shirt, "My darling, beloved Oz, you are alive! I feared the worst, but we are together again and will never be parted!"

Oz patted her back and crooned, "There, there, darling. Everything is all right now. Don't cry, I'm here. I'm here."

"Yes, yes, everything is all right now." She wiped her face and let out a short laugh of relief. "I should have never doubted that you would live to rescue me. You are so brave and strong, and you love me so dearly, you would endure anything, renounce anything, to save me and marry me."

"Er, well, yes. Of course." Oz kissed the top of Ravenna's head and patted her back again. "Of course. What else?"

"Oh, but you are in terrible danger!" She pulled away and gazed at Oz, her beautiful face distorted with fear. "Knox Bloodworthe is here!"

"Bloodworthe? Here on this island?"

"Yes, not far off, the way I came. Oh, Oz! He means to kill you the moment he sees you. I've seen the bloodlust in his eye, he will stop at nothing!

Oz steeled himself and pushed Ravenna away. He took up his sword. "He'll not succeed. I've killed better swordsmen than he. I will prevail."

Ravenna threw her arms around him again. "You must prevail! I cannot live without you! I thought I'd lost you, and I nearly died. Without you, I truly would die!"

He held her with one arm while the other hand gripped his sword, his eyes scanning the jungle's edge. "Don't talk of dying. I will defeat Knox, and we will be together always."

"Yes, yes, always."

In the quiet that followed, Oz felt Ravenna's breath change. No longer gulps for air between sobs, it slowed and deepened. She tightened her hold around his body and slid her hands lower. The press of her against him, with only the light fabric of his shirt to cover, affected him. She gave out a quiet moan against his breastbone and held him tighter. His nethers tingled and his manhood began to respond.

She let her hands slip to his buttocks. "Darling, you're without your trousers."

"Yes, um, yes. I was... bathing."

She squeezed and pulled at his haunches to grind him against her. He was erect now and could not help pushing back and basking in the tantalizing sensations.

She let out a short, throaty laugh. "Bathing? Funny, but you smell somewhat of fish."

"Ah, yes. I hadn't yet finished" he stammered. "Hadn't really started, truth be told, when I heard your calling."

"Oh, well, that's no matter." She looked up at him with lidded eyes of desire, now pressing her body brazenly against him and shifting right to left against the swollen object of her lust. "We can get dirty now, and bathe together later."

She reached under his long shirt and gripped his cock, her smile now broad and bright and her eyes dancing with wicked abandon.

Oz dropped his sword and froze, again of two minds.

No! shouted the one, *you must be married first!*

Are you joking? countered the other, *do you see a priest anywhere? Marry her by fucking her!*

We must observe the proper ways and ceremonial rites.

Proper ways? He fucked a fish!

Not a fish, a mermaid. More cetacean than fish, actually.

You're quibbling. He didn't marry the mermaid, but boy, did they ever—

The customs are different here.

Really? You're going to hang your argument on cultural relativity?

Ravenna broke up the captain's silent debate. "You'll find that I've learned a great deal about how to please you, dear husband."

"You... you have?"

She lowered herself to her knees, slowly, watching his face. "Yes. I want to be the source of your utmost joy." She lifted his shirt. "Perhaps this will give you a glimpse of what awaits you in the conjugal bed."

Oz watched, transfixed, as Ravenna slowly passed her soft lips over the head of his now rock-hard member, then ran her tongue along the sensitive underside. He groaned, making the lady chuckle in triumph. That sent crackling vibrations from his loins up along the network of nerve endings to his scalp, lifting every follicle of his hair like he'd been struck by lightning.

She drew his stalk further into her mouth, sucking it gently at first, then harder.

Blood left the captain's brain and rushed southward. Lightheaded, he swayed gently. Ravenna used his motion to advantage. With her free hand she pulled on his hip, drawing him in deeper, then pushed back so he nearly withdrew. She pulled him in again, moaning and making faint sounds of slurping, then pushed him back.

She glanced up and laughed again on his bulging, throbbing pillar, delighted to see the captain's eyes roll back and his mouth gape with astonishment at the onslaught of sensation.

Without conscious intention, he took over the rocking action, thrusting slowly into the lady's mouth, withdrawing and thrusting again. His face remained blank as his body obeyed the forces of nature, pushing deeper and pulling back farther with every swing.

It heated Ravenna's blood to feel Oz enjoy her in this way. She'd practiced with the stone replicas a thousand times in convent. But the real thing, pulsing and throbbing against her tongue, giving such obvious pleasure to her beloved, thrilled her as she'd never known. She now sucked hungrily, groaning with every push and pull.

A few more strokes and she could wait no longer.

She threw herself on her back, lifted her skirts and spread her legs, shouting in a hoarse whisper, "Now! Now my darling, my beast, my husband! Fuck me now, hard and mean and do not stop until you fill me with your hot, salty spunk!"

Oz stood there, swaying like a palm tree in a gentle breeze, his member diamond hard and flushed red below the purple head, devoid of rational thought. He watched the lady before him, vigorously rubbing her raised, reddened love nub with one hand and torturing her breast with the other, crying out in animalistic grunts interspersed with a few human words, every part of her body and mind and heart inviting him to take her in the intimacy ordained for marriage—

Marriage.

The thought shocked Oz awake like a backhanded slap.

"No" he croaked, taking an unsteady step back.

"Yes!" the lady shouted.

"No, darling, no, we—"

"Fuck! Me! Now!" the lady grunted, plunging two fingers in and out and kicking her heels in the air.

"Ravenna, my darling, please! Until we are married, we have sworn before God that we will never—"

Ravenna gave up her self-abuse and broke into racking sobs, hands covering her face. She cried until her lungs emptied, drew a deep ragged inhale and sobbed louder.

Oz stood and watched her, wanting to offer solace, wondering what he could say or do while he withheld the one thing she wanted that he felt he could not give.

As she quieted, he knelt beside her. "My darling Ravenna, I am so sorry, but—"

The slap shocked him for its surprise, fury and power. He fell back and sat in the sand, held his cheek and stared into the face of the terribly angry, frustrated, headstrong woman with incandescently beautiful blond locks.

"What *is* it with you *men*?" she growled, her face red and her forehead a chevron of angry, scowling contempt. "The sisters taught me that men are horny as goats and want sex every waking minute of every day!"

The word caught the captain's attention. "*Men?*" he whispered.

"But no matter what I do, how attractive I make myself, however much I fling myself at their feet, no one will touch me!"

Their feet? Oz mused. *No one?*

She suddenly crawled to where he sat and took his face in her hands, staring into his eyes. "Oz, listen to me. We are betrothed, which means our union is already blessed. By my parents, by the church, by God. We are married in every sense save one, having the rites of marriage spoken and our vows witnessed."

He smiled and held her hands. "Yes darling! Yes, and as soon as we get home we will shake the priest from his bed if need be and be married immediately! I swear this to you!"

"No, you don't understand. We may never leave this island. It is cursed, and there is a terrible monster killing and eating anything it can catch."

"Yes, dear, but we'll find a way—"

"No!" She drew back from his grasp. "We can't be certain! We may very well die before sundown. And I would die without ever knowing the joy and beauty of our union. You are my husband, in every way, yet you deny me that which I most want! How can you do that?"

"Because I love you. I don't want to defile you."

"Defile me, damn you!" she screamed. "As your wife I order you to defile me! I want to be defiled! I need to be defiled! Do your duty as my love and my husband and fuck me like a two-ducat whore!"

"Darling, please, you're far too upset to know what you are saying."

Ravenna's scream, head back and open throated, pierced the very sky, making Oz cringe and cover his ears.

She stood and shot fire from her eyes into his. "To hell with you, weak-spined man-boy! If you lack merely the courtesy, let alone the courage to do what's right, then our wedding is off, and for all I care you can go straight to hell!"

She turned to go back the way she came and stopped, unbreathing, staring at the jungle's edge.

Oz caught sight of what had made the lady freeze like prey under the eye of a tiger. He scrambled to his feet, found his sword and stood, staring as motionless as she.

"Oh, Oz is surely going to hell, dear lady" said Knox Bloodworthe, drawing his rapier from the scabbard at his side. "And I am he come to do your bidding and send him there."

Chapter 16 - Don't Say We Didn't Warn You

For a breathless moment the tableau held; Knox standing at the edge of the clearing, sword in hand, the sharp tip pointing to the sand; Oz, naked save for his long white shirt, already in a stance of defense, his blade seeking the foe's left eye; Ravenna between the two, mouth agape and hands held out as if to stop them both with her will.

Oz broke the silence. "It is you who will take his rightful place in the inferno, Knox Bloodworthe. You could not best me at sea, you will not do so now."

"Look into my eyes, Ozymandias Wembleye, and see there my conviction, my vow to the sea gods, that you will wet my blade with your heart's blood, and I will watch with joy as you breathe your last."

"You're both fucking idiots!" screamed the lady.

The men faltered and stared at Ravenna.

"What?" mumbled Knox.

"Beg pardon?" said Oz.

"Idiots! Fools! Numb-skulls! Dumb as a box of dildos! We have to all work together or we'll all die here!"

"Preposterous" spat Oz.

"Never" answered Knox.

"Just hear me out." Ravenna pulled at her bodice with one hand, showing considerable pale pink cleavage. She then lifted her skirts with the other, revealing her long, smooth legs to her thigh crease. "Take me, both of you. Together or not, I don't care. Take all your frustrations out on me and end your hatred through love. And orgasm. Lots of orgasm. Come in me, on me, near me, anything. But let me break this spell of rage and vendetta through the physical act of love. Then we can combine our efforts to escape this terrible island."

Both men gazed with puzzled frowns at the lovely woman still sporting the most agonizingly shiny, long, healthy hair, despite all she'd been through.

"Darling?" Oz ventured, "did you perchance partake of some potentially poisonous fruit or fungus in the jungle? You've been acting very strangely today."

"Indeed" said the pirate. "Quite the slutty idea for a so-called *technical* virgin."

Oz scowled. "Technical?"

"Never mind" Ravenna hurried to say. "Well?"

Knox shook his head. "I told you that I would never touch you because, *if* we return to Hudson, I must give you back as the virgin I kidnapped to get my ransom. I am a man who keeps his word."

She turned to Oz.

"As am I, my love. The vow of chastity until marriage I made to you, to your parents and to God must not be broken."

"Men" Ravenna scoffed, "bah! Fine, go ahead then, and I hope you both die. The world will be a better, less stupid place!"

She made her way, grumbling, to the edge of the clearing between the two men and folded her arms. "Well? Get on with it!"

Oz again took up his defense, knees bent, rapier aimed at the pirate's eyes.

Knox frowned. "Put your pants on, Oz. I'll not duel a man with his dick flapping about."

"You will not strike while I am defenseless?"

"On my honor." Knox stuck his sword point into the ground and stepped back.

"Very well." Oz stood his sword in the sand and went to the rock where he left his clothes.

"Your boots too" shouted the pirate. "I want to kill you fair and square, without any advantage. None will say Knox Bloodworthe cheated."

"Cheated?" Oz laughed as he pulled on his dark blue trousers. "You've cheated, lied, stolen, and killed since you could walk. You are the worst of the worst. I'll rid the world of you and be hailed as a hero!"

"Hero? Oz the ambusher, Oz the killer of women? A hero?"

The captain sat on the rock and pulled his boots on. "I did not agree to the killing of Bonnie, Knox. I told Argo it was wrong. I was after you, but we captured her. I could do nothing!"

"Liar! You could have saved her, could have helped her escape and live. You knuckled under to that murderous duke, you lackey, you bum-licking slave!"

Oz stood, hurried to his sword and took it up. "It is no matter now, murderous scum. I will finish the job I began when I lured you to that armory, to end your villainy once and for all!"

Knox grabbed the hilt of his rapier and screamed, "The job is mine to finish, dog!"

Ravenna shouted, "Enough with the overwrought dialog, you twits! Is this a duel or some hack writer's wet dream?"

The men glanced at the lady, then met eyes and sprinted to join in battle.

Despite her snarky preamble, Ravenna gasped at the fury of the two men as they met and flailed at each other, blades flashing and ringing out with each speedy thrust and parry. Back and forth they advanced and retreated, neither gaining an upper hand, matched in skill. Circling, Oz lunged in a desperate attack only to be beaten back. Knox growled and charged Oz with a flurry of feints and a killing slash, missing the captain's throat by an inch.

From the west side of the clearing Ravenna heard voices and saw the two pirate sailors emerge from the foliage, swords and daggers drawn. Squid followed, pulling Adelaide by the arm.

From the opposite direction came Bilge, also with blade in hand. "Captain Oz! I'll fight at your side!"

"No!" Oz backed away from Knox, panting, his sword held out to keep him at bay. "No Bilge, this fight is mine. Only I can finish it."

Knox shouted over his shoulder, "The same goes for you lot! No one is to touch Oz or help me. I will have my vengeance on him myself. Let no man join the fray!"

Tim suddenly landed on a low branch to Ravenna's left, startling her. "I say, they both appear to be quite adept at the Art of Arms, don't you think?"

Ravenna only stammered, too frightened to speak.

Tom appeared on another branch to her right. "Who gives a fuck about those assholes?" he snarled, "Hot tits here is all I wanna look at!"

The lady gasped at the second monkey, identical to Tim save for his foul mouth.

"Now, Tom" Tim chastised, "do please mind your manners with the lady, will you, hmm?"

"Shit, you're insufferable" Tom groaned. "You should have been the one to team up with *pater* there, not me. You two are made for each other."

While the simian siblings argued, Ravenna watched, transfixed, as the man she loved, or thought she loved, and the man she thought she hated, but could perhaps love, fought desperately to kill each other.

She gave out a gasping scream when Oz lost his footing under a fierce assault and fell backward into the water of the lagoon. Knox held back, waiting until the captain regained his stance before he waded in and pressed his advantage. The men panted, grunted, and cursed as they became more desperate.

Oz took first blood, finally piercing the pirate's shoulder with a shallow stab, only to take a riposte slash to his sword arm. The torn shirt revealed a sweeping cut across his bicep that splattered drops of blood as the captain parried and countered the vicious onslaught.

Now knee deep in the water, Oz broke off and scrambled to get to dry land, Knox close behind stabbing and slashing. Both men could barely catch breath before they were at it again. Ravenna could see triumph in Knox's eyes, his rage now in full flame, as Oz's arm slowed and barely fended off each blow.

Knox finally beat the rapier from the captain's grip, disarming him. The lady screamed again when the pirate kicked Oz onto his back and stood over him, blade poised at his heart.

Gasping for air, voice low and raspy, Knox growled, "What has been stolen from me will be returned a hundred-fold!"

A roaring screech pierced the air, stopping the breath of eight people and two monkeys.

From the edge of the jungle a massive green monster broke through behind the two pirate sailors and roared again. Though shaped like a man, it stood towering over the pirates, its huge jaws wide and filled with rows of jagged, razor-sharp teeth. The green skin was scaled armor, and a ridge of sharp plates ran in a jagged line down the back from the neck to the end of a long, meaty tail.

Its muscled arms reached out and gripped one sailor around his trunk as the jaws clamped shut over his entire head and shoulders before the man could so much as shout.

Wrenching and pulling, the monster gnawed the man into two ragged, bleeding halves. It gulped the man's head and chest down into its throat.

The beast threw the lower half aside and clutched the second sailor who stood stunned and maddened by the sight. Squid hurried Adelaide away as the mighty lizard-thing held the screaming man like a rag doll and bellowed its roar. It lumbered into the clearing, revealing its lower body with huge, powerful legs, between which a four-foot-long engorged, arrow-tipped and razor-barbed appendage waved and slapped against the thighs with every step.

Six people and two monkeys watched in silent horror as the monster impaled the man on its beweaponed lizard-schlong once, twice and thrice, tearing and shredding the flesh of his lower body with every thrust. Still alive until the fourth stabbing, the man screamed his unendurable agony, then finally gave out his last cry as a great vomitous gush of fouled blood.

The hideous monstrosity threw the pulpy remnant of the man aside and sprinted toward Ravenna. Still in shock, no one moved, no one spoke or gasped or cried out. In seconds, the monster crossed the clearing, caught Ravenna in its giant bloodied hands and kept running, crashing through the jungle.

Five people, helpless as newborns, stood staring at the trees and bushes still waving after the monster's exit, silent and breathless. The roar of the beast and Ravenna's screams echoed and faded away.

Tim and Tom jumped down from the branches, landing on either side of where the lady had stood and now was no more.

Tim addressed the stricken people. "Kalakuta, ladies and gentlemen, Kalakuta."

Tom grinned brightly. "Monster-God of the island, folks, Kalakuta! What a performance, let's hear it for him!" He began clapping loudly and whistling.

Tim clapped softly and delicately. "A first-rate performance, I'd say. One for the books. The old boy hasn't lost his game after all these years. A *tour-de-force*."

"Whatta guy!" Tom shouted and whistled again. "What say, folks? Give it up for the one, the only, Kalakuta!"

When they finally stopped clapping and shouting, the two monkeys folded their arms and said, in unison, "Don't say we didn't warn you."

Chapter 17 - A Change of Command

The tableau of stunned faces held for a long moment as Ravenna's plaintive screams died away.

Squid stood on one side of the lagoon, staring blankly as he held the crying, shivering Adelaide. Bilge, face drained of color and mouth agape, stood on the other.

Knox still towered over the fallen Oz, his only movement shallow and rapid breathing as he stared at the jungle foliage still waving after the exit of the monster. Oz lay on the ground, now rolled over on his belly to witness the lady carried off.

He was first to act, pushing himself from the ground and running toward the jungle. "Ravenna! I'll save you my love! Ravenna!"

This spurred Bilge into action. He sprinted to intercept his captain, using his superior weight and strength to capture Oz and subdue him.

"No, sir, please!" he begged, "You'll do no good, just get yourself killed!"

Oz struggled against his first mate's bear hug. "Damn you, Bilge, let me go! That's an order!"

"No sir, not 'till you've gained back your senses."

Knox roused and stumbled toward the jungle, his legs strained from the fight, sparking Squid to chase and tackle him to the ground. "Take it easy sir" he said, "don't go off bein' foolish."

Adelaide approached the knot of people, her arthritic legs unsteady in the deep sand, crying openly with a kerchief held to her mouth. "My dear girl! Saint Salacious preserve her!"

Knox, on hands and knees, dropped his head and cried. "Oh, Ravenna."

The captain shifted his anger from Bilge to the pirate. "What are you crying for, you bastard? All you've lost is a ransom. I've lost the love of my life!"

"She's not" Knox mumbled.

"Not what? Not the love of my life?"

"No. She's mine."

"Yours?" shouted Oz.

"What?" gasped Bilge.

"Cap'n?" quizzed Squid.

"Mine. I didn't know until I saw her taken away, but now I realize, she is my soul mate." With that, the proud pirate let himself collapse face first into the sand and weep.

Adelaide said nothing as she passed out and fell over backward.

Another tableau held for some time of four stricken men and one unconscious woman.

Tom burst out in loud laughter. "Ha ha ha! Oh, what fools these assholes be! Ain't nobody gonna be nobody's love, except maybe Golden Girl and the Jolly Green Demon. Old Kal's gonna come back soon and belly up to the people buffet. He'll turn you all into lizard shit right quick. Ha ha ha!"

"Now, Tom" chided Tim, "these poor folks have had a frightful time and are more in need of cheering up than being force-fed lurid descriptions of the terrible fate that awaits them."

"Okay. Hey folks, cheer up. You ain't monster chow yet!"

Still struggling in the arms of his first mate, Oz screamed at Knox, "You filthy, rotten bastard! If you so much as touched her I'll—"

"Wait!" Knox shouted, lifting his head and revealing his reddened, tear-stained cheeks. "Foul-mouthed monkey. What was that you said, about Kalakuta?"

"Um, let's see." Tom scratched his head and made a puzzled face. "You mean that part about him stuffing his gullet with you all like so many sausages?"

"No. About someone being his love."

"What's this about, pirate scum?" Oz fumed.

"It's about saving Ravenna, you perfumed fop. Shut up!" He again eyed Tom. "Tell us."

"Oh, nothing, nothing" Tom said, hands behind his back and rocking on his feet, eyes wide and feigning innocence.

Tim tisked. "Tom, in the interest of fairness I think you should tell them."

"Tell us what?" Oz said, "whatever it is, I *demand* you tell us."

"You ain't in a position to demand anything, *pater*.

Tim harrumphed.

"Shit. Okay." The abusive anthropoid sighed. "I guess it's no harm you knowing, since you'll all be dead soon. Kalakuta ain't gonna kill the girl."

Four male voices said "No?" with varying accents of surprise.

Adelaide, starting to stir, mumbled, "Lumpish, fool-born barnacle."

"No" Tom giggled. "It's really kinda funny, you see—"

"Tom?"

"Okay, dammit. The big, freakish reptiloid has a soft spot for blonds."

"Aye?" said Squid.

"Aye, salty."

"A soft spot, you say?" inquired Bilge.

"Yeah, that's what I say. Clean the wax outta yer ears, bilge rat."

Knox growled, "Enough!" and leapt to his feet, sword in hand, taking Tom by surprise. The rapier's tip rested against the monkey's throat before he could dodge.

"Spill your words and be quick or I'll spill your blood."

Tim held up his little black hands and said, "One moment, if you please Mister Buccaneer, sir. I will explain."

"You do that" said the pirate, "while I hold your little friend here hostage. Deal?"

"Acceptable terms." The erudite monkey cleared his throat. "Kalakuta kills and eats anything and everything he wants."

"Don't forget about the raping" Tom said, before feeling the sword tip dig into his flesh and going quiet.

"But there seems to be one sort of creature he won't kill and eat ... or rape ... and that is a blond woman."

"How's that?" asked Squid.

"It's odd, I know, even a bit difficult to believe when you've seen how he works. But it's true. We've had quite a few shipwrecks wash up on these shores over the years. A few of them resulted in blond women surviving. Kalakuta captured them each in turn, but never killed them. He just... just..."

"Just *what?*" shouted Knox.

"Looked at them."

Four male faces stared at the monkey with mouths open and brows furrowed.

Having sat up, awake and listening, Adelaide spat, "Ruttish horn-beast."

"No, good lady, he attempts no untoward advances. He just ... looks."

"Just ... *looks?*" ventured Oz.

Tim nodded. "Yes. He gazes at them with wide eyes like a swooning lover, making quiet little cooing noises. He's beyond smitten. He practically worships them."

Knox said, "Do you mean he has them still, these blond women?"

"Oh no. The rest are all dead."

"I thought you said—"

"He doesn't kill them. He chains them up and gazes at them lovingly, burbling and sighing, until they die of starvation or kill themselves by dashing their heads against a rock."

Adelaide slumped backward again, out cold.

Tom giggled. "Hee hee, yeah. Then he gets all sad, moaning and crying like a baby, pushing their emaciated bodies around with his finger, trying to wake the little things up. It's fuckin' *adorable*!"

Oz threw off his mate's hold and shouted, "Then we can still save her!"

"Oh sure, Captain Stupid" snarled Tom. "You and your little troop of tender meat sacks can just march right up to his lair, stamp your little feet and say *Give us blondie!* I can't wait to watch that short-and-sweet battle of the boneheads."

"There's a way." Oz looked at each still conscious face. "Kalakuta has a weakness! There is a magic talisman hidden in a cave somewhere on this island. If we find it, we can defeat him and rescue Ravenna!"

"An' how is it yer knowing about this, then?" inquired the old salt.

"Uh ... well ..."

Tom looked wide-eyed at the captain, then grinned. "I thought I told you not to go looking for—"

Oz pointed. "Tom told me!"

Four sets of eyes shifted to the smutty monkey.

"Wha-what?" he sputtered.

"Tom told me all about it. It's a magic totem pillar made of a rare stone. It's in a cave guarded by a magician, or something. Right, Tom?"

"No, man, no. There's nothing like that on this island."

Tim tisked again. "Come now, Tom. Let's be good sports about this."

"But they don't stand a chance in hell! Even *with* the damn thing."

"True, but you don't want to spoil their fun, do you? We've been through this before."

"Aww, shit. Fuck it. You tell them."

"Very well."

Five pairs of eyes watched Tim, Adelaide having partially recovered, sitting slack-jawed in the sand.

"There is indeed a cave where a magic talisman is hidden that could — *could*, mind you — be used to defeat Kalakuta."

"Do you know where it is?" asked Knox.

"Yes."

"Can you take us there?" asked Oz.

"Can" Tom said, "but won't."

Tim said, "I will lead you there."

"Shit!"

"You can stay behind, Tom, if you wish."

"Naw, I'll come. Don't want to miss the blood-spattered fun."

"Wait." The pirate swung the tip of his sword to point to Oz. "There's the matter of our duel to settle. I won, fair and square. I had you under my blade when Kalakuta attacked. You'd be dead now, but for that beast."

Oz walked toward Knox until the tip of the sword rested against his breastbone. "What will you do then, villainous scum? Will you just run me through, standing here, in cold blood? Is that your idea of fair and square?"

The pirate's face twisted with anger and confusion. "If you agree to stay away, and let me rescue Ravenna myself, I will let you live."

"Not on your worthless life."

"I won't fight you again, Oz. If you refuse this, I'll kill you where you stand."

Oz raised his chin. "She is my greatest love. I'll not abandon her."

Knox pressed his sword tip into the captain's flesh, making him wince. "She is mine! Surrender her to me!"

Oz leaned into the pain of the sharp blade. "Death first!"

So consumed were the two captains in their fury, and so vigilant were the mates to their leaders' danger, that none of the four men noticed the little nun stir and approach.

She stepped unheeded between the combatants and delivered a vicious uppercut blow to the pirate's testicles.

Knox went cross-eyed and dropped his sword, clutching his ruptured jewels with both hands.

Oz watched Knox collapse in the sand until Adelaide turned and likewise slammed her tiny fist into the underside of his ball sack, so fiercely that Oz felt his gorge rise in his throat as he toppled over.

The two powerful men lay writhing on the ground, gripping their swelling gonads, groaning and spitting out dribbles of acrid vomitus.

The sailors stood watching their commanders' agony, paralyzed by the knowledge that they could do nothing to help, lacking anything remotely usable as an ice pack.

"Thou currish folly-fallen barnacles!" she shouted, taking a moment to spit at each in turn. "Cockered, rump-faced canker-blossoms art both of thee! You stand here measuring your cocks while dear Lady Ravenna is in mortal peril by the evil whims of that hell beast! Fie on thy dankish, malt-wormy souls!"

Tom whispered to Tim, "I like her. She has spunk."

"Now hear me, miscreants." Her voice low and measured, she commanded all attention. "No more will you care for your blood feuds, nor your so-called honor, nor even your worthless, rotten lives. We will, all of us, join forces with only one purpose and sacred duty, to save the lady."

She gave Knox's rump a solid kick. "Am I clear, thou spleeny, toad-spotted haggard?"

"Yes" groaned the pirate.

A boot in Oz's kidney drew a loud groan and a saliva-flecked cough. "And thou, idle-headed baggage?"

The gurgle from Oz's throat approximated an affirmative answer sufficient to Adelaide's liking.

Saying nothing, she pointed to Blige with a withered finger and an evil eye.

"Yes ma'am."

She turned the finger on Squid.

"An honor ta serve ye, Sister."

She spoke to Tim. "When these whey-faced, hurlish, hell-hated strumpots can walk, lead us to the cave."

"Yes, Sister Adelaide."

She pointed to Tom.

He saluted. "At your command Admiral, with one request."

"What is it, filthy bugbear?"

"Kick 'em again!"

———— ⧈ ————

Chapter 18 - The FuckKnuckles Quandary

The little group trudged through the jungle for more than two hours, Adelaide leading the four men, following Tim and Tom who leapt from branch to branch in the canopy.

The still limping Knox growled, "How much farther?"

"Not far now" Tim answered.

"Good thing, too" muttered Oz. "I don't think I can stand any more blasted chattering from the monkey twins."

Tom laughed. "You'll change your tune when The Big K is scarfing down your bloody carcass, *pater*. This is the *fun* part of the whole trip."

"Tim can lead us" Bilge said, "so I may still make you into a hat."

"Try it, bilge breath. You'll be wearing two pounds of monkey shit instead."

"Quiet!" shouted the nun. "Thou pox-laden canker-blossoms will awaken the beast and lure him to kill us all. Be silent!"

Bilge mumbled, "Yes'm."

Squid sidled alongside Adelaide and whispered in her ear, "I loves ya when yer angry, pet" and pinched her bottom.

The nun gave the pirate a backhand that sent him to his knees. "I'm not your pet, thou rank, onion-eyed measle." She walked on without looking back.

Rising as the other men passed by, Squid sighed and whispered, "Ah, but ye are, dear sea goddess, ye are."

Tim stopped to watch a moment. "True love. Isn't it inspiring, Tom?"

Tom scoffed. "If that's what people call true love then I'm glad all we do is screech and fuck and throw shit at each other. I don't get how people manage to stand their own kind." He moved on to the next branch.

"Well, to each their own" Tim said, and followed his twin.

Behind Adelaide, Knox and Oz had jockeyed back and forth for the lead spot the whole way, grumbling and pushing each other like schoolboys in a lunch line.

"I don't know what you're thinking" Oz said, pulling the pirate by the shoulder to step ahead. "Ravenna would never love a blackguard like yourself. You're deluded if you believe that."

"Ha! You don't know her at all, you fop." Knox elbowed his way past Oz. "You should have seen how she threw herself at me."

"Liar. If you so much as kissed her cheek it was by force." The captain tried to push Knox aside but could not budge the larger man. "And I swear I'll kill you if you touched one golden strand of her hair."

"I refused her, you effeminate man-child. She begged me to take her, and I didn't. Now that I know she is my true love, I'll give her what she wants, what she needs, what you could never provide!"

"Double liar." Oz grabbed a handful of the pirate's long dreadlocks and pulled his way ahead, making Knox cry out in pain. He hurried to take the lead. "Ravenna is chaste as chaste can be. She's pure as spring rain, untouched as the snow-capped peaks of the highest mountains. She would never—"

"Do you know about the dildos?"

Oz stopped in his tracks and turned to face Knox. "What dildos?"

"The sculpted schlongs she's been plunging into her pretty pussy for a year now." Knox stood toe-to-toe with the captain and grinned. "Under the instruction of the cursing nun up there."

"Triple liar."

"It's true, isn't it, dear Adelaide?"

"You logger-headed louts" she mumbled as she turned back to join the fray, "enough with your foolishness! Do you want another hard knock to your collective yarbles?"

Oz turned to plead, "Is this true, sister? What this bastard says about Ravenna?"

"Oh, what of it?" she answered, waving her hand in dismissal. "It was all just part of her training to be a good wife to you, so what are you worried about? She loves only you and she knows how to please you. You should be grateful to Saint Salacious."

"Ha! You hear that, Knox? She loves only me. So, even if she has... um... shall we say, *practiced*, she has done so in preparation for our nuptials. You will never have her love, or, well... anything else of her."

Again Knox grinned wide and white, a gleam in his eye. "But you will not bed her until you have the sanction of marriage, correct?"

"Correct. It is only proper."

"Then you will lose whatever esteem she still has for you. Being without her precious pretend pricks since I took her from the *Bentley* has left her worked up into a frenzy, in need of a good, hard cock ride. She wants it from me, and I intend to give it to her."

"You'll not, scum!" Oz laid his hand on the hilt of his sword. "I'll kill you first."

Knox mirrored the captain's stance. "I should have run you through when I had the chance. But you'll not— gah!"

The pirate and the captain both stared in wide-eyed terror at the little nun standing between them, hands gripping them both at the crotch of their pants, squeezing their still-sore testicles just enough to silence their curses and get their attention.

"You'll not endanger the lady's life another minute with your squabbling, thou vain, idle-headed varlots." She quickly closed her fingers tighter around their balls and nodded. "Agreed?"

The men squeaked out, "Agreed" in unison.

"Hey, meat-sacks" shouted Tom from a high branch, "we're here!"

"Here?" Bilge said, "where?"

"At the cave, Bilgey."

Squid squinted into the canopy. "But Tim just said we were close, an' we've not taken ten steps since. How did we suddenly get *there*?"

Tom jumped to a lower branch and balanced as it swayed. "Plot convenience" he said, winking.

The four men and one woman looked one to the other with puzzled frowns.

Tim landed on the branch with Tom and gestured. "Just through this thicket, folks. Follow me."

They followed, and once the tall ferns and low-hanging vines cleared away, they faced a mighty stone cliff sheered away near the ground. As they approached, they saw that the broken section formed a deep cave barely tall enough for a man to pass through.

Peering into the dark, Adelaide said, "Tim? You said a wizard guards this cave?"

"Indeed madame. Not a great wizard, mind you, just a sort of second-tier conjurer, but the job is not particularly difficult, so he's just barely good enough for—"

"Hey!" came a high-pitched voice from the depths of the cave. "Don't bad-mouth me, you stuck-up simian!"

The men all drew steel.

"Who's there?" demanded Squid.

"Show yourself!" shouted Knox.

"Come out now!" growled Bilge.

Oz began, "In the name of—"

"Alright, alright!" came the answer. "Keep your collective pants on, people, sheesh!"

A man, or an approximation of one, ambled into the light. Barely four feet tall, the green skin of his face was deeply wrinkled, and he sported large, lobed ears and a few scraggly hairs on his head. He was covered throat to feet in a dark robe of rough fabric.

"It's just like you lot" he said, squinting against the brightness, "you come along all full of yourselves and demand that I jump to your orders. The arrogance! I'm here in my cave, minding my own business, just doing my job, and next thing I know it's all 'Come out' and "Do our bidding!' and 'Help me I've been bitten by a swamp spider!' No manners, no manners at all these young folk, I tell ya!"

Oz stepped forward. "Are you the wizard who guards the totem pillar that can defeat Kalakuta?"

"That and a few other trinkets. I try to stay stocked for the tourist trade."

"What is your name, wizard?"

"Handjob."

In the silent moment that followed, Tom snickered. "I love this part."

"Handjob?" asked Bilge, the one of the group most knowledgeable in such matters.

"It means something else in my language."

Knox asked, "What does it mean?"

"It means, *Best Friend*."

Bilge nodded and mumbled, "Sounds about right."

"That's not important" said Oz, "we are in haste. Our beloved Lady Ravenna has been carried off by Kalakuta. Will you give us the talisman to defeat him?"

"Give?" Handjob scrunched his face. "Whoo-boy, listen to you, mister give-me-whatever-I-want when-I-want-it-for-nothing. Sheesh! Doesn't anybody know common courtesy anymore?"

Knox asked, "What can we give you? We have nothing."

The little man winked and placed a finger by his bulbous nose. "If you can answer my riddle, I will give you the talisman."

"What riddle? Tell us!" Knox said.

Handjob cleared his throat and tried to affect a sonorous, important-sounding voice, but managed only a baritone squawk. "Two trolls are playing FuckKnuckles, and they play five games—"

Oz wrinkled his brow. "What in blazes is FuckKnuckles?"

"It's a game. So they play five—"

"How's it played?" asked Squid.

"Well, you start by holding out your fists, knuckles up and—"

"Enough!" screamed Adelaide. "It doesn't matter how it is played! Shut up and let the witch ask his riddle."

"Wizard, madame."

"Get on with it, venomed skainsmate!"

"Yes, ma'am. So, two trolls are playing FuckKnuckles. They play five games, and each wins the same number of games. How is this possible?"

The men looked at the little man a moment then to one another.

Handjob smiled with haughty pride. "Answer thou this puzzle clever, and I will help with thy endeavor."

"Heavens" Oz said, rolling his eyes, "bad poetry to boot."

The wizard spread his hands. "Well? Many have tried but all have died."

The men mumbled in thought.

"Five games."

"Same number of, five divided by two, uh..."

"There was a draw!" Knox shouted.

Startled, Handjob said, "What?"

"One of the games was a draw, a tie! So they each won two games!"

"Hmm, I never thought of that."

"Then give us the talisman."

"But it isn't right."

"Oh."

The men went back to grumbling their confused thoughts.

Having stood among the stumped men all this time, arms crossed and foot tapping, the little nun finally groaned, "Thou beslubbering, bootless, spongy, tottering, dizzy-eyed, motley minded, tardy-gated apple-johns! None of you has brains enough to pour piss out of a boot!"

Watching their puzzled faces just made Adelaide all the angrier.

"They weren't playing each other!"

Even more shocked than before, Handjob whispered to the nun in awe, "That's correct."

"Of course it's correct ye weak-pated moldwarp!"

"It's just" stuttered the wizard, "nobody has ever guessed it before!"

"None?" asked Oz.

"Not one in twenty years. Dozens have come to me, looking for the secret to defeat the monster. Not one gave the right answer. Until now."

"Well then" said Knox, grinning, "this must be a high day for you. The fulfillment of your great purpose."

"No" said the sad little man, eyes to the ground. "It's rather a bit of a let-down, truthfully."

"Show us the talisman, then" sighed Adelaide, "weepy, sniveling boy-child."

"All right, follow me."

As the disappointed diviner led the party into the cave, Tim whispered to Tom, "I knew the answer. Did you?"

"Of course, it's the stupidest riddle in the world."

"And we've never helped any of the others, all these years."

Tom smiled. "Why spoil the fun?"

Tim smiled back. "Indeed. Shall we go in?"

"After you."

"No, I insist, after you."

Cutting short their usually hour-long ritual, the two monkeys joined arms and strode into the cave together.

Chapter 19 - Sword in the Stone This Ain't

T he men bent low to enter the mouth of the cave while Handjob and Adelaide walked upright, all carefully picking their way as their eyes adjusted to the gloom. Around a bend they saw the orange flicker of firelight and entered a large, high-ceilinged cavern lit by torches set in stanchions on the walls.

Long tables and cabinets of ornately carved wood stood end-to-end around the room, each heaped with a dazzling display of treasure. Jewel-encrusted golden goblets and ewers, trenchers and vases crowded the tops and shelves, each piled high with heavy necklaces and bracelets, crowns and rings, the looted riches of a hundred kings strewn about without care to catalog. Several chests of iron-banded wood stood open, overflowing with gold coins and bullion, rough, unset jewels and pearls the size of a man's eyeball. Swords and daggers, pikes and halberds, bows and arrows from an array of foreign lands, enough for a small army, stood leaning against a wide corner, followed by shields and helmets and armor of wood and metal and leather, each decorated in symbols and totems of warrior clans.

Handjob waved his arm and gave his visitors a proud smile. "Keeping the talisman to defeat Kalakuta is just a side-hustle. This is my main gig."

The pirate's eyes gleamed with avarice. "Where did you get all this booty?"

"The Merfolk bring it to me."

"Merfolk?" quizzed Adelaide, "you mean, fish people?"

"Not fish so much as cetacean. Like dolphins or whales. Sea mammals."

"The Mermaids we sailors tell of" Squid said, grinning, "they're real?"

"Yes, Mermaids and Mermen and Merwomen and Merchildren. A whole race of them lives around the island. When storms send ships to the bottom of the sea, they like to gather up whatever treasure they can find. They're like children that way, fascinated by shiny objects. Some keep a few baubles to wear, but they have no use for most of it, so they bring it to me."

Oz listened nervously to the talk of the Merfolk, wondering if the little wizard knew anything of his tryst with Eve. To pretend ignorance, he asked, "These Merfolk sound either generous or naive. Or stupid?"

"No, they're wonderful. So nice, kind, and peaceful. All they do is play and sing and make love. At least, they did until the monster came. They're just generous, and like I say, what use do they have for this stuff?"

Knox asked, "What do you do with it? Trade?"

"Who with? We only get people from shipwrecks. Before Kalakuta came, I'd give them whatever they wanted, but then they'd get jealous and take sides, one group fighting the other until they killed themselves off. Now I give people the weapons to fight Kalakuta, but it's useless. Only the talisman can kill him."

The nun's eyes widened, "Then why didn't you give them the talisman?"

"I told you. No one answered the riddle. I don't make the rules."

"Fine" Knox said, his voice sharp with impatience. "We answered your riddle, or the nun did, anyway. So give us the talisman."

"Sheesh, look who's all high-and-mighty. Without it, you'd be nothing but a quick snack for the Big Green Guy, sonny, so how's about a little courtesy?"

The pirate laid his hand on his sword hilt. "Give us the talisman, now!"

Tim and Tom, taking turns adorning each other with bracelets and crowns, both laughed.

"My, my" Tim said, "no matter their predicament, people always seem to be full of themselves, don't they?"

"Got that right. Even with their woman carried off and horrible death staring them in the face, assholes to the end, every one of them."

Handjob bowed. "Sure thing, Hotspur. Since you ask so *nicely*."

The wizard produced a key on a lanyard from under his robe and went to a large ebony cabinet on the far side of the cave. The five people and two monkeys watched as he slipped the key into the lock, turned it and opened the two doors. First Knox, then Oz, Adelade and the sailors slowly approached to gaze on the wonder that made them gape their mouths and hold their breath.

The inside of the cabinet was black as the outside. The large, erect jade phallus within, propped on a stand so that its prominently ridged head pointed skyward, glistened in the flickering torchlight. The stone was deep green with rivulets of white and black streaking the length like bolts of lightning. Carved to anatomical perfection by some master of the art, it modeled a man's appendage perfectly but for the color, the smooth, reflective polish and the size, longer and thicker than the average man's at full rigidity. It stood on a base of two massive testicles, veined and swollen as if ready to pour forth man seed enough to populate a kingdom.

"Saint Salacious, preserve us" breathed Adelaide.

"Aye, there's a lady pleaser, ta be sure" said the grinning old salt.

Bilge nodded and raised an eyebrow with appreciation. "A tadger for the ages."

"Ravenna would love that" whispered Knox.

Oz scowled at the pirate. "What?"

Handjob gestured to the crystalline colossus and proclaimed, "Behold! The only thing that can destroy the monster Kalakuta!"

"How?" asked Knox.

"Hmm?"

"How does it work?"

"Ah, yes, it has instructions." The wizard used the key to open a small drawer in the cabinet, took out a scrolled parchment and handed it to Oz.

The captain unfurled the paper and read aloud. "To he who would slay the beast Kalakuta, greetings and salutations. This, The Rock Cock, provides the only means by which mortal man can defeat the demon. Heed well these instructions."

"The Rock Cock" said a smiling Tom, adjusting a crown around his middle like a belt. "Good name."

Tim nodded. "Someone hired a very good marketing consultant."

Oz unrolled the paper further and continued reading. "First, thou shalt find a virgin, be they man or woman."

"A virgin?" said Squid.

"Man or woman?" queried Adelaide.

"Captain Oz!" exclaimed Bilge.

Caught by surprise, Oz said, "What? Me? Oh, yes, um..." he thought back to how his day began. "Yes. I mean... um hmm?"

"You're a virgin?" asked Knox, stifling a chuckle.

"Yes. Well, technically."

"*Technically?*"

Oz ignored the pirate's question and read on. "Next, thou shalt speak the magic word, *spunkdrizzle*, three times, no more, no less. Three times thou shalt say *spunkdrizzle*, and the number of times thou shalt say *spunkdrizzle* shall be three. Speak the word not less than three times, nor speak the word more than three times, for two and four are numbers that are not three."

"Holy spunkdrizzle" Tom whispered to Tim, "Couldn't they find a decent copy editor for this junk?"

"Probably a translation problem" his twin answered.

"Ah."

"Having spoken the magic word three times only, then the virgin shall rammest The Rock Cock fully within Kalakuta's poop chute, who, being a very naughty boy, shall die very badly and forever."

After a moment, Knox said, "This must be some sort of cruel joke."

Handjob frowned. "Oh no, the instructions are quite clear."

"They are clear yes, but ridiculous!"

"Well, you know how magic is" the little wizard said, trying to lighten the mood with a smile.

Adelade chimed in. "No we don't, foul windbag of dank fumes. You could enlighten us."

"Magic works by working. I know it sounds as if some horny hack writer had a few too many happy lilies, but the spell and the talisman work together to focus the energy of the person casting the spell. If you believe in the magic and follow the steps perfectly, it works!"

Oz scoffed. "Balderdash."

"It's true!"

"You are claiming, little magician, that due to my status as a man who has not yet enjoyed a bit of rumpy-pumpy with a lady, I must be the one to casually stroll up to that man-eating monstrosity and give him the old *How's Yer Father?* with a lithic lingam? And that repeating a made-up rude word three times will keep me from harm and destroy the beast?"

Handjob nodded. "Exactly."

"How did you come to have this talisman?" asked Knox.

"Kalakuta had it with him when he first got here."

Oz threw his hands in the air. "Gods! This gets more absurd with every minute."

"Not absurd" Handjob corrected, "magic. If the hero must overcome a magic monster, that hero needs magic to do the job. I took the cock and hexed it to defeat him. It's necessary!"

Tom whispered to Tim, "Sounds like another bit of plot convenience to me."

"More like plot contrivance, this is" Tim answered.

"What's the difference?"

"The convenience is Kalakuta's weakness. The contrivance is The Rock Cock."

"Ah."

"An' why didn't ye destroy the beast yerself?" asked Squid.

"What? You think I can't get laid 'cause I'm short, green, bald and ugly?"

Adelaide said, "If you tried to touch me I'd skin you alive and sew myself a stylish man-leather jacket."

The little wizard laughed. "Darling, I know how to give a woman what she wants and some things she doesn't want but discovers she likes."

"Pah" scoffed the nun, "hell-hated pig-dog."

"Well, Oz" Knox said, "it looks like this is the only way to save Ravenna. I'd do it myself, but I'm far from being virginal." The pirate grinned wide and bright. "Far from it."

"We'll all help, captain" said Bilge.

"Aye! We'll take some of those pikes" offered Squid. "Surely we can distract the beast a moment and give you a chance."

Adelaide folded her arms. "You must do this, Captain Ozymandias. For Ravenna's sake, you must."

"I will fight at your side, for Ravenna." Knox declared, hand over heart.

Oz straightened his spine and took a deep breath. "Very well, though I am certain I will end up as the entrée on Kalakuta's lunch menu, I must do whatever I can to save the lady."

"Save her for me, you mean" muttered Knox, *sotto voce*.

Oz strode to the cabinet and lifted The Rock Cock. "Oh, my. That *is* heavy."

"'Heavy is the hand that holds the cock'" Handjob misquoted.

"Follow me" Oz commanded and started for the exit.

Knox fell in next, carefully nudging Adelaide aside. The sailors took pikes and long swords from the wizard's treasures and fell in behind.

"Wait!" shouted Handjob, "I must go with you!"

The train stopped and regarded the little green man.

"Why?" asked Oz.

"Well, wouldn't you like me to show you where his lair is?"

"Oh, yes. Yes, please." He bowed and gestured for the wizard to take the lead.

Oz pointed to Tim and Tom. "Monkeys? Take the rear guard."

As the group marched from the cave to face the massive lizard beast Kalakuta, Tom shouted, "Looks like you're gonna be the one doing a little *rear-guard action* today, *pater*!

Oz ignored the laughter of the twin monkeys while Knox clamped his hand over his mouth to hide his smile.

Chapter 20 - Luncheon of the Monster Party

Ravenna woke with a start to the sigh of gentle waves and the tang of salt in the air.

She found herself laying on a large, flat boulder of wet, black stone. The rock rose from the center of a lagoon that let out to the sea. She remembered the lagoon where she found Oz, but this one opened into the ocean, and here, a rock bridge connected the center stone to an outcropping on the edge of the jungle. The water encircled the island, but she could walk to the sandy beach from where she lay.

She stood and made ready to do exactly that when the clank of iron and a tug on her leg stopped her. An iron cuff on her ankle connected to a long chain embedded in the center of the rock. The bridge led to freedom, but the taut chain and the cuff that bit into her delicate flesh denied her all hope.

Her long, flaxen hair had finally suffered some dishevelment, with wet tendrils hanging over her face and some of the ends slightly frayed. She smoothed it back and tied it in a large square knot to protect it from further damage. Her azure gown was torn at the sleeve and shredded at the hems, but she was otherwise unharmed.

She turned in a circle to take in her surroundings. The impenetrable jungle blocked her view toward the interior of the island. The saltwater inlet surrounded the rock island and opened into the sea. She stared out looking for land or the mast of a ship, but the water and the cloudless, sun-drenched sky met at a horizon with no visible line. The beach ran as far as she could see in each direction and curved away out of sight.

The little girl who never cared for church fell to her knees and clasped her hands over her closed eyes.

"God, I know I should have honored you better, but I am scared and alone and I need help. Please Lord, I swear I will renounce the world and join a convent if you will deliver me from this terrible place. I will be celibate — I mean that, really, truly celibate. I'll never so much as finger myself again, I swear. I will give all my devotion to—"

A piercing man's scream stopped her breath and drew her eyes to the sea. Just beyond the shoreline a man, bare chested and waist deep in the water, thrashed and screamed before some unseen power pulled him under. Ravenna stood and peered at the whirling water, her hands at her mouth. When the man surfaced again so did Kalakuta, gripping the victim in his powerful hands. Several wounds in the man's chest bled freely, inflicted by the beast's taloned fingers. The monster carried him inexorably toward the lagoon, rising in the water as it reached the shallows, until Ravenna could see the man's lower body was that of a fish, or a porpoise, she corrected. He struggled to break free but was powerless in the giant lizard-man's grip. He screamed again, but gurgled out a stream of blood as Kalakuta tightened his grasp, crushing the man's ribcage.

Barely alive, the merman lay limp in the monster's arms, twitching and gasping as Kalakuta brought him ashore and made for the lagoon. Ravenna watched in horror as the beast took a large bite from the man's midsection, then pulled and shredded away a chunk of flesh and organs as casually as she might take a bite from an apple. As it made its way over the narrow rock bridge to where she stood, it took the man's head off at the neck with one swift snap of its jaws. She could hear the heavy bones of the skull crack and crackle in its mouth as it chewed and swallowed.

Ravenna backed away, her trembling legs near to buckling, to the far side of the rock until the chain tightened and held her. Again falling to her knees as Kalakuta drew near, she clinched her hands together and prayed to the demon as if to an implacable, revengeful God, able only to stutter two words, "Please no please no please no!"

When he stood only a few feet away, Kalakuta stopped and sat down on his haunches, holding the remains of the merman in one hand like a child's doll. His black, fathomless eyes stared at her as he tilted his massive head to one side, then the other. She watched him settle himself to sit on one hip and rest on the arm that held the pulpy carcass, like a man on a picnic blanket ready for a repast. As he gazed at her, she heard him utter a low, quiet sound, a gurgling or rumbling that reminded her of a kitten's purr.

For some moments they held the tableau; the beautiful blond girl kneeling before the gigantic, scaly abomination as it held the bloody remains of a magical creature in its powerful, taloned hand, gazing on her with the fawning deference of a love-stricken boy unable to muster the courage to ask the girl for a dance.

Kalakuta then took hold of one of the body's arms and easily pulled it away like the drumstick of a well-roasted chicken. He tossed the bloody limb toward her, careful to land it just within her reach.

Ravenna regarded the long, well-muscled arm before her, some portion of the shoulder joint still intact and peeking white from the mess of red gore. She shuddered at the thought the beast was offering to share his meal.

When she looked on him again, Kalakuta tilted his head, gurgled, cooed, and seemed to soften his face into the reptilian shadow of a smile. He pointed with his free hand to the arm, then to her and cooed again.

She glanced at the offered meat, then at the giant. "For... *me*?"

He burbled again, a sound so soft and gentle she could barely believe it came from the hideous creature. He then plucked the other arm from the torso, held it by the hand and plopped it into his mouth, chewing on the bicep as one would nibble an ors d'oeuvre at a cocktail party.

Believing she might find some means of escape in this strange turn of events, Ravenna took up the arm in both hands and smiled at her benefactor. "Thank you."

Kalakuta finished shredding the last of the flesh from the limb, picking at smaller sinews to get every morsel, then tossed the bones over his shoulder into the water of the lagoon. He burped and gurgled his contentment, looking over the remaining torso and tail for where he might bite next.

She waited until the monstrosity glanced her way again, then brought the arm near her mouth and pretended to bite and chew. She saw pleasure rise in what had seemed his dead, soulless eyes. She smacked her lips and said, "Mmm, that's delicious," exaggerating her enjoyment like a mother trying to trick her child into tasting a vegetable.

Kalakuta looked again on the corpse, made his decision, gripped the body by the tail and bit off a sizable portion of the merman's flank.

With a moment to think, Ravenna wondered at her lack of disgust over the bizarre scenario, concerned it had something to do with the state of her soul. Regardless, it gave her a slim chance at survival and escape. Glancing at the long, razor-bedecked member laying casually on Kalakuta's thigh gave her the idea that her fortunes lay with the skills she'd learned from the Sisters of Saint Salacious: flattering and inflating a man's ego to make herself the source of his pride and joy.

Again she smacked her lips, then set the arm down, saying "Truly delicious, but I couldn't eat another bite." She patted her tummy for theatrical effect. "Thank you so very much."

The colossus finished chewing the meat and swallowed, then tossed the last shreds of the carcass into the water. Still laying on his elbow, he nibbled and slurped at his fingers to savor the last tiny morsels of meat and the blood that slicked his hands.

When he settled his gaze on her again, Ravenna smiled brightly. Kalakuta again tilted his head, his eyes glistening, and gave out a new purr, higher pitched, trilling like a songbird. She undid the knot of her hair and arranged it over her shoulders, finger-combing it as best she could to smooth the tangles and restore some shine. The monster's eyes widened; the trilling increased in speed and pitch. She lowered herself to sit on one hip and propped on her elbow, tugging at the hem of her gown to show her shapely legs to the knees.

She noticed the phallus throb slightly as Kalakuta's voice dipped lower.

Just like any man, she thought. *Can't enjoy a bit of conversation before his cock is standing for the queen. I can't go too far down that road, but at least I know very well the part I play in this game.*

She redoubled her smile and toyed with some strands of her hair. "So, tell me about yourself. What sort of pursuit entertains you when you're not cruelly killing and devouring Merfolk?"

The trilling dipped and rose in a slow, simple melody and he again leaned his huge head to the side, eyes locked on her.

"Badminton? Playing the harpsichord? Croquet?"

The beast either hiccuped or chirped.

"Croquet, is it? Oh I adore croquet. All those heavy balls clacking about, the revenge shot sending your foe's ball to a far corner. It's thought to be a genteel pastime, but it is in truth a blood sport."

His cooing quieted and his eyelids drooped, as if she sang a lullaby.

She took the sign. "Let's sing together, shall we? Do you know *The Farmer's Daughter and the Tired Old Priest*? I'll teach it to you."

She drew a deep breath and sang:
Far from his parish the old priest went riding.
He stopped ev'ry traveler and gave them a chiding.
So to rescue their souls all their sins he decried,

Accusing them all of Greed, Lust, and Pride.

The massive lizard man quieted and lowered himself, resting his head on his arm without taking his eyes from Ravenna. His breathing slowed.

Then the old priest arrived at a simple man's farm,
Whose daughter beguiled him with beauty and charm.
When the priest did dismount, she brought him cool water,
And he fell for the spell of the farmer's young daughter.

Kalakuta closed his eyes.

Yes, she thought, *sleep you colossal brute. Sleep until I wake you. Which would be never.*

Chapter 21 - Never Fuck with a Little Man

The day's heat under the thick jungle canopy filled the air with the humidity of a steam bath as six people and two monkeys made their way across the island. With Handjob in the lead, followed by the captains, the nun and the sailors, they sweated thorough their clothing and wheezed labored breaths.

Tim and Tom traveled high in the treetops, easily following while enjoying cooler air and the occasional snack along the way.

"Don't you pity the poor two-legs?" Tim asked, stopping to bite into a ripe pooka fruit.

"Pity?" scoffed Tom. "Fuck 'em. They were stupid enough to evolve, lose their tails and body hair? They deserve whatever they get." He pulled down his own pooka and took a large bite.

Tim said, "You have a very big mean streak."

"And you" Tom said around a mouthful of fruit, "have a very small cock."

Oz glanced up at the chattering laughter from the simian siblings, then said, "How much farther?"

"Not far" Handjob said. "Listen. Hear the ocean? Kalakuta makes his home in a lagoon on the beach."

Knox said, "How is it you know so much about Kalakuta?"

"Well, he's been a special project of mine since he got here, twenty years ago. I told you I found him—"

"Yes" Oz said, "shipwrecked, like us?"

"Like you, and not quite. First, he was no ordinary man. I never figured out exactly what he'd been, but he'd had some magic, that was certain. While he was in the sea, trying to make it to shore, some sort of creature stung or bit him, and the venom was already turning him into the monster he became. I got him under some shelter and tried to nurse him and reverse the venom, but it was taking over fast. He grew by an inch or more every hour, busting out of his clothes as his skin turned green and scaly. While he could still speak, he insisted the dildo would cure him, and he kept ramming it up his bum, desperate to stop the pain of his changing."

Bilge nudged Squid and said, "I've heard tall tales at sea, but this is one for the ages."

"Just wait 'til I get going! Where was I?"

"Self-inflicted buggery" said Squid.

"Ah, yes. For hours he cried and groaned as he changed, cornholing himself with that jade schlong, while I tried spell after incantation after hex, none of it working. Things got to the point where I could tell he was beyond help. He'd lost the ability to talk, reduced to shrieks and growls, unable to understand me or respond to my questions. Then his body developed spines and talons and his eyes went all black as his head morphed into something between a snake and an alligator. So I gave up, grabbed the dildo and ran off to save my skin."

Oz remembered what Eve said about how Kalakuta became the destroyer of the Merpeople, soon to wipe them out. He pushed Handjob from behind, growling, "Then you're responsible for all this, aren't you?"

"Me?"

"Yes! You could have killed him while he was vulnerable. Instead, you tried to cure him and let him grow into the beast that will wipe out all the Merfolk. You're to blame!"

The little wizard stopped, turned and punched Oz in the belly, dropping him to his knees. As the captain fought to draw breath,

Handjob pointed and said, "I'm not the monster here, fuck-knuckle. I was trying to save a man, or a magician, but still a man. He became what he is because of some freakish accident with a sea creature, and I could do nothing to stop it. But I was damned if I was going to just give up and let him die, let alone kill him with my own hands. Are you that kind of monster, captain? Would you kill someone you had a chance to save?"

"Actually" Knox said, looking down on his rival, "he did."

"Damn you, Knox" Oz wheezed, finally catching his wind, "I told you I didn't kill Bonnie, and I could do nothing to save her."

Knox sighed. "So you say."

Handjob knelt and scowled at Oz. "You think I didn't regret what happened? Twenty years now I've been powerless to stop him, watching him kill the Merfolk and the people who wash ashore here, hearing his blood curdling roar and the screams of his victims. So that's why I hexed the dildo, and created the only magic that can defeat him. To make up for what happened, for what I could not have stopped. So at least my conscience is clear, captain. Is yours?"

After a few moments with only the sound of the far-off waves and Oz's labored breath, the little magician stood and whispered, "I thought not."

Knox asked, "Why did you use the phallus for your magic? It seems a strange way to deliver a spell."

"It was precious to him. He believed it would save him, and even though it was completely useless, he was certain it was his salvation."

For once, Adelaide's stern face softened with puzzlement. "How does that give it the power to destroy him?"

Handjob smiled at the nun. "Because madame, false ideas, or more to the point, our belief in them, are always the source of our undoing. A drowning man who believes only God can save him will refuse the rescue line thrown from shore and perish."

After a few seconds of silence, Tom, sitting with Tim on a nearby low branch said, "Wow, man. That's heavy, gran'pa. Did you write that while you were tripping balls on happy lilies, all one with the world and shit?"

Tom and Tim cackled with laughter until Handjob pointed two fingers their direction and blinked twice.

The monkeys both grabbed their crotches and screeched in pain as a puff of smoke flashed from each of their white, furry ball sacks. They fell from the branch, thudding on the ground and writhing there, groaning.

Handjob smiled at the stricken primates. "Here's an old saying that I just made up. Never fuck with a little man. He'll kill you."

Adelaide had wandered away from the men, straining to hear a faint sound over the susurrating waves. "Listen! Do you hear something?"

Handjob, Knox and the sailors joined her as Oz stood and held back, rubbing his belly.

After they heard a wave crest, crash to the beach and recede, a faint melodic sound, high and sweet, reached them. Adelaide recognized the voice.

"Ravenna!" she gasped and ran toward the sound.

Knox caught the nun in his arms and covered her mouth with his huge, callused hand. "Shh! We can't go running in not knowing if Kalakuta is there, or Ravenna's state."

Adelaide stopped struggling and nodded.

The pirate captain released her, turned back to the men and whispered, "Follow me, and be silent."

The little troop did so, with Oz at the rear, leaving Tom and Tim behind to nurse their wounds.

They approached a clearing where the foliage thinned, and the beach came into view. Before they left the last of their cover, Knox held up a hand and motioned everyone to stop and spread out beside him.

They formed a line along the jungle's edge and knelt, pulling back at the fronds and vines that separated them from open ground.

Every breath stopped and every heart skipped at the sight of Kalakuta, reposed on the slick black rock at the center of the lagoon, head on his arm and cooing like a sleepy baby as Ravenna sat before him, singing sweetly:

So the lesson, dear traveler, is easy to see.
The sin you abhor lives the strongest in thee.
If you'd shrink from the hell that lying makes hotter,
Then heed well the wisdom of the farmer's young daughter.

Somewhat recovered, Tim and Tom landed on a nearby branch.

Tom whispered, "Aww, ain't that abso-fucking-lutely *precious*?"

Handjob pointed over his shoulder and clicked his tongue. The faint whiff of burning hair and quiet squeaks of pain brought a smile to everyone's lips.

"I didn't say anything" gasped Tim.

Chapter 22 - In the
Rough Without a Wedge

After the group watched the tableau of monster and maiden for a time in stunned silence, Bilge whispered, "Orders, captain?"

"A moment, Bilge. My mind is racing with tactical possibilities."

Knox frowned. "And who says you're the captain to be giving orders?"

"Certainly you wouldn't suggest yourself?"

"Why not?"

"You are not a naval officer. You are nothing but a pirate."

"A pirate who bested you with steel. Who bested you at sea."

"You never! We were overtaken by the storm."

Knox's eyes glittered. "Liar. You were halfway sunk by the time—*yow!*" The pirate flinched and grabbed his bicep.

Oz likewise yelped, "*Ouch!* What the? —"

They turned to find Adelaide, flashing a tiny dagger she had long concealed at their eyes. "Next time" she growled, "it goes in your necks."

The men rubbed their wounded arms, blood soaking into the white cloth of their shirts, grumbling.

"You'll be wastin' no more time or breath arguing who's got the bigger dick" the old nun hissed. "You'll listen and do as you're told." She thrust the blade at Knox's eyes.

He flinched. "Yes'm."

When she pointed the tip at Oz, he cowered with his hands up in surrender. "Of course, dear Adelaide."

She pocketed the dagger. "Good then. Now, the bridge to the rock is on the other side of the lagoon. Oz and I will stay here while the rest of you rogues sneak through the jungle to the far side. When we see you in place, Oz will swim quietly to the rock from this side. Can you do that lad, and slip by the beast?"

"Yes. I will remain submerged until I can hide at the rock."

"Good." She pointed to the three others. "When I see him ready, I'll signal. You all rush to the edge of the bridge, making a ruckus and brandishing your weapons. Get the monster focused on you."

Squid smiled. "I know you don't love me, pet, but this is a harsh way to say so."

Adelaide's eyes twinkled. "If ye live, I'll let you call me *pet*, but not before."

"Aye, commodore."

"Oz, when they have Kalakuta's attention, you climb up on the rock and do the deed."

"Preferably before we are all killed and eaten, please." said Bilge.

Everyone passed uneasy smiles, one to the other.

Handjob blurted. "I can help!"

Oz said, "I thought you were powerless to defeat him."

"To defeat him, yes, but I can help distract him."

"How?" asked Knox.

"With this." The height-challenged magician reached into his robe and held up an ornate hairbrush of filigreed gold with fine boar bristles.

Squid chuckled. "Will you groom him to death, then?"

"You all saw how he is with the lady, yes?"

Everyone nodded, Squid still quietly laughing at his own joke.

"He treats all blond women the same way. When I brush my hair with this, I will create a magic disguise of myself as a beautiful blond girl. He will fall under my spell and become docile."

"A brilliant plan" Oz said, "if you had more than..." he pretended to count, "three and a half hairs on that green, pock-marked pate of yours."

Handjob stink-eyed the captain. "It's the brushing that counts. It creates the illusion of the woman that Kalakuta will see, not me as I am."

Knox said, "It's worth the try, ask me. Adelaide?"

"Yes, we all must do what we can. Thank you, wizard Handjob."

The little magician grinned with delight.

Knox picked up his halberd and said, "Then we're off."

"First, a prayer." Adelaide folded her hands and bowed her head.

Slowly, unaccustomed to the ritual, Knox, Squid, and Bilge lowered their eyes and clumsily pressed their palms together.

Oz dutifully clenched his eyes shut, performed an odd sequence of hand-touches to his forehead, knees, nipples and nose, then clasped his hands together.

Watching from a high branch, Tim made prayer hands and nudged his brother, who stuck the middle fingers of each hand into his nostrils.

The nun whispered in reverent tones, "Beloved Saint Salacious, I beg of thee, save these brave men from a terrible, agonizing, soul-shattering death. If they must die, let them leave this world as quickly and painlessly as possible. Amen."

The sailors frowned and eyed each other as they gathered their weapons and moved off into the jungle.

"Not a very inspiring invocation, was it?" mumbled Knox.

Squid grinned and said, "No, we'd be better off with a good curse."

Adelaide and Oz waited and watched for the men to reach the far side of the clearing. When she saw Knox wave, she nudged Oz, who quietly crept to the water's edge and slipped beneath the surface.

The monkeys found a vantage point high above the action but hidden behind densely leaved branches. Tom broke a small stick from the branch and held it to his mouth, whispering. "Well, ladies and gentlemen, here we are on the final hole of this incredibly rough course and the players are all in for the big win. I'm Tom with the play-by-play, and my brother, Tim, is here to give you the color commentary."

Tim found a stick for his own mime. "Thanks, Tom, it's great to be here on this hot, humid afternoon with the going solid underfoot and very little sign of rain."

"Tim? Do you think we're in for more of the horrible, bloody mayhem we saw earlier today, when Kalakuta reduced two minor players to mounds of shredded flesh and goo?"

"The team can't take another loss like that, so we can only hope for a minor miracle. Maybe the new replacement, Handjob, can pick up the slack."

"Well, it looks like the players are in place and ready for the next round, so let's watch."

Adelaide saw the captain surface at the rock and waved to Knox on the far side.

Knox tightened his grip on the tall halberd he carried and whispered, "All right lads, here we go."

"Wait" Handjob said, "don't go rushing in yet. I'll go first, get him all googley-eyed at the beautiful girl, and then you come in to baffle him."

Knox looked to Squid, then Bilge. Each of the men shrugged.

"Very well, little wizard. Good luck."

Handjob smirked with pride. I don't need luck. I have magic." He began running the brush over his head, first with one hand, then the other, crooning in a sing-song voice, "I'm just an innocent girl, a lovely girl who means you no harm. Yes, all I am is..." As he brushed and spoke, he left the cover of the jungle thicket and did the best imitation he could of a young girl strolling through a garden.

Kalakuta did not notice the newcomer for a moment, so enrapt was he in blissful attendance to Ravenna's beauty and singing. But as Handjob reached the far side of the rock bridge, Ravenna heard him, stopped her singing and stared, wide eyed, at the little man.

The three men in the jungle watched as well, their faces registering the same shock as the lady.

"It's not working" gasped Bilge.

"Gods of the deep, no" whispered Squid, "he's... he's..."

"He's just himself" Knox said.

Kalakuta turned to follow where Ravenna stared, caught sight of the intruder, and growled a terrible, low rumble in his massive chest.

"Oh, my, what a lovely day to be a beautiful young girl without a care in the world" sang the little wizard, appearing to everyone as himself, a short, fat, green, bald old man. "I certainly hope I don't meet up with any terrible monsters on such a fine day."

"Handjob!" Knox hissed, "come back! It's not working! Come back!"

The monster slowly rose to his feet and glared at the little wizard, the rumbling growl growing louder and saliva beginning to drip from his grimacing lips.

From his high redoubt, Tom said, "Oh dear, we're off to a disappointing start, Tim. This is a par five hole with a wicked dog leg right and Handjob seems to have chosen a pool cue for the tee off."

"Worse than that" Tom added, "more like he's going to take a swing at the ball with his own John Thomas."

"You said it, Tim. This is going to hurt, big time."

Oz took the opportunity to peek over the rock. "Psst!" he whispered, making Ravenna turn and beam a smile when she saw him. He held a finger to his lips and shushed her. She crawled to the edge, leaned over and kissed him.

"Thank you dear, but no time for pleasantries. We're rescuing you."

"You are? Wonderful! How?"

"With this" he held up the jade phallus.

The lady eyed the impressive totem. "That might make me feel better, dear Oz, but how will that rescue me?"

"It's not for you. It's for him." He pointed the dildo at the monster, now drawn up to his full height and winding up to pounce.

Ravenna glanced at Kalakuta, then at Oz, her face twisted with confusion.

"No time, dear" Oz said, "as soon as the little wizard succeeds, I will spring into action."

"Succeeds?" Ravenna said. "At what?"

"He is distracting the beast. If a virgin can bugger the monster with this, he will die."

"Really? Who told you that ridiculous story?"

"He did" Oz said, pointing the green cock at Handjob, "the little magician."

"La, la, la-dee-da" the wizard kept singing, "I'm so happy to be a lovely, young, blond girl." He continued brushing his bald, green head, still looking every bit as what he really was, and not one iota like that of a lovely, young, blond girl.

The three men, still hiding in the foliage, were now shouting, "It's not working! Run away! Run away!"

But Handjob remained confident in the efficacy of his magical skills right up to the moment when Kalakuta gripped him around the trunk with both of his clawed hands and raised him into the air.

As his ribcage was crushed, his voice lost all little-girl qualities and sounded more like the burbling rush of rotten yogurt being expelled from a bota bag.

"Uh-oh" Tom said, "looks like he's shanked that one into the trees."

With a mighty roar, the monster slammed the little man's body down on his erect, bladed cock, three times in rapid succession, tearing the entrails out through gaping wounds between his legs in a shower of blood and gore.

"Holy horror show!" shouted Tom. "The little green wanker is *toast!*"

While the beast impaled the now thoroughly dead wizard another time, then bit his head off, Oz climbed up on the rock and shouted, "Spunkdrizzle! Spunkdrizzle! Spunkdrizzle!"

Kalakuta froze. He moved not a muscle, still holding the remains of the little man in his hands, the skull and a length of the upper spine in his clenched jaws.

For a second, the world did not move. Six people and two monkeys stared breathlessly at the immobile creature.

Adelaide shouted, "Oz! *Go!*"

Shaken from his stupor, the captain ran forward, knelt, peered under the tail to find the target and with a mighty grunt shoved the Rock Cock as deep into the brute's cloaca as he could manage.

The violation of his nethers shocked Kalakuta back to life. He tossed Handjob's ragged remains into the water, then swung his mighty fist and knocked Oz into the lagoon. Ravenna gasped and watched as Oz submerged, surfaced again spitting water and gasping for breath, but disappeared again as if pulled under.

Kalakuta reached under his tail, extracted the jade phallus and tossed it aside. It clanked on the rock platform and rolled to within Ravenna's reach. She made to pick it up but stopped and gagged at the foul stench and sight of the now shit-befouled pillar.

The colossus roared and beat his chest, not one whit impaired by the attack, let alone dead.

"It didn't work" whispered Knox.

"The beast lives" gasped Bilge.

"How can that be?" said the old salt.

On the other side of the lagoon, Adelaide's face turned red with anger as she gnashed her teeth and grumbled, "Who's ewe didst thou tup, thou ruttish, fen-sucked codpiece?"

"What do you think, Tim?" Tom said into his stick. "Double bogey? Triple?"

"As many bogeys" said Tim, "as there are grains of sand on the beach."

Chapter 23 - A Kiss Before Dying

Still hidden in the foliage, Knox and the sailors stood frozen with shock and fear. They watched Kalakuta turn right and left, scanning the jungle's edge and sniffing the air in search of more intruders. The little wizard's blood still stained the monster's jaws as he breathed low growls and flexed his taloned fingers.

Bilge finally found his voice and whispered, "Permission to run away, sir?"

"No, fool" Knox hissed. "We still must save Ravenna."

Squid said, "How? The spell didn't work."

Knox fought a moment to calm himself and think rationally. "It might have failed because Oz is no virgin."

The old salt furrowed his brow in confusion. "He claimed he was. Who would lie about such a thing?"

"A man betrothed who must hide his indiscretions from his wife-to-be."

"Ah, yes." Squid turned to Bilge. "Well? You know him best. Has he dipped his wick or not?"

"Never. My captain is a man of his word."

"He could have done the deed and hidden it from you" Knox said.

"That is true, but—"

Knox held up a palm, silencing Bilge. "It's the only chance we have."

"We?" Squid said. "If Oz was no virgin, then who?..." Squid stopped himself and turned to follow where Knox was staring. Behind

Kalakuta stood Ravenna, the Rock Cock lying near her feet. "But cap'n, ye can't mean—"

"She's a virgin."

"So *she* says."

Bilge interrupted. "She's been a year in convent. She is pure as the driven snow."

"I wouldn't go *that* far" Knox said, his face taking on a leering grin, "but pure or not, she's our last chance."

As the men watched, Ravenna talked quietly with Kalakuta, drawing his attention back to her. She spoke as if to a child in a tantrum, softly and sweetly, toying with her long, beautiful hair and batting her eyelashes. The monster turned to stare at her, cooing and purring, tilting his head like a faithful puppy waiting for praise.

Knox handed his halberd to Squid, stepped a way out of the jungle and waved to get Adelaide's attention. She waved back. He gestured broadly, pointing to Ravenna and Kalakuta, then bent over and pointed to his own bum.

The nun shook her head and shrugged her shoulders, arms out and palms up in an exaggerated mime of *What are you on about?*

Again the pirate pointed at the lady, then the beast. He raised his arms, affected a wide, teeth-baring grimace and bent over again to point to his behind, then thrust his fist upward several times, slapping his bicep with the other hand.

Adelaide's face lit up with understanding as she flashed a thumbs up.

Knox rejoined his men. "All right then, here's the plan. We'll run out there and threaten the monster, not too close, to distract him. Adelaide will tell Ravenna to do what Oz did, and we can only hope she'll do it and that she really is a virgin. Or we're all dead."

"We're all dead either way" Bilge said, "sooner or later."

"Aye" said the grinning old salt. He slapped his new friend on the back. "Best be brave about it and laugh in Death's face."

"Good lads" said the pirate.

The three sailors steeled themselves, gripped their weapons and nodded their heads. Knox shouted, "Now!" and ran into the clearing, Bilge and Squid on his heels. The miniature army stopped at the far end of the bridge, snarling and shouting oaths, jabbing the air with their spears.

Kalakuta turned to face them, crouched and ready, the jagged edge of his razor teeth on full display. He bellowed his terrifying roar, ready to pounce.

Adelaide ran into the open, waving her arms and shouting, "Ravenna! You must do as Oz did, it's our last chance!"

Ravenna turned and saw the little nun running toward the lagoon. "What?"

"It is a spell to kill the beast! A virgin must ram the jade dildo into his arse!"

"You mean, that thing?" She pointed to the Rock Cock.

"Yes! Do it! It's the only way to kill him! Only a virgin will succeed!"

Ravenna stood a moment, thoughts racing.

Over the shouts of the sailors, she heard Knox. "Ravenna, my love! If you really are a virgin you are the only one who can defeat Kalakuta!"

"What do you mean, *if?*" she answered, hands on hips.

Knox screamed, "Please! We'll all die if you don't!"

The green colossus roared again and took a menacing step toward the men.

"Hmm" the lady mused, "I'm not sure it wouldn't be better if you did die."

"Please! I'll give you anything you want if you'll save us!"

Her face softened into a sly, Cheshire grin. "Anything?"

"Anything!"

"Help us, dear Lady Ravenna" the nun shouted. "You're our only hope!"

The huge beast roared again. The screech snapped the lady out of her reverie. As Kalakuta seemed ready to attack, she ran to his side and pointed at the shouting sailors. "Stop! Come no closer. Let him be!"

Shivering with fear, Bilge gave out a grunt of surprise.

Squid breathed, "Heh?"

Knox, likewise, "Uh..."

Kalakuta turned to gaze upon the blond woman's stern face, rumbling an upward inflected gurgle that seemed to say, in language only a twelve-foot, bipedal lizard monster could understand, *What the fuck?*

"Go away, all of you" Ravenna said, her voice low and commanding. "Leave us alone. I belong to Kalakuta now, and I won't let you harm him. Go!"

The men stared, spellbound.

The nun gaped at the scene, unbreathing.

The brute cooed at his beloved, his black, fathomless eyes glistening.

Ravenna tried again, affecting a sing-song voice. "I saiiid, go awaaayyy now, so he and I can be alooone." When no one moved, she stage-whispered, "We need privacy so we can... you know..." She finished with a wink.

Knox finally caught her meaning. "Yes" he said, backing away and gesturing to Bilge and Squid to do the same. "We're going now, please don't hurt us. We'll leave you alone to... um..."

His voice trailed off as he and the sailors disappeared back into the jungle.

Kalakuta's coos and trills rose and fell in a gliding melody as he gazed on Ravenna, clasping his hands at his breast like a devotee in a saint's shrine.

"Come dear" she said, taking him by one massive, taloned finger, "let's rest together and I'll sing again for you."

She led him to the center of the rock and motioned downward with her palm, like she'd learned to do when training a dog. She made the gesture a few more times before he caught on and laid down on his side, eyes fixed on her every move.

"There's a good beast" she murmured.

Watching from behind the leaves and vines, Squid whispered, "Ye don't think she actually means to—"

"Impossible" snorted Bilge, "she'd be killed."

Knox smiled. "She'll not be killed. Watch."

Ravenna strolled casually toward the edge of the rock, humming a tune. She caught Adelaide's eye and waved her away. The little nun scampered back to her hiding place.

Still humming, Ravenna wandered slowly to where the jade dildo lay, steeled herself and held her breath. She knelt and picked it up, then leaned over the edge to swish it in the water of the lagoon. Several wipes finally cleaned it, the lady gagging between breaths and finally rinsing it of the last filth with her delicate, white hands.

She glanced at Kalakuta, laying on his side and using his hand to pillow his head, gazing at her with undivided attention and endless devotion. She began to sing.

My only true love has left me alone.
To another's soft arms my lover has flown.
No one hears as I cry, and my sad state bemoan.
How I wish that my soft heart would harden like stone.

Still crooning, she stood and sauntered toward the beast, staring into his glistening black eyes, testing the heft of the phallus in her hands.

No more will I weep; no more will I sigh.
If my love loves again, then again so will I.
I've a long life to live, or tomorrow may die.
So today I will love; with a new love will lie.

Knox heard sniffling and glanced at his men, both rugged faces wet with tears and their lips quivering. He felt his own heart ache, the dull pain creeping toward his throat.

"'Tis a beauteous sight to behold" sniffled Squid.

"Aye" whispered the pirate. "She is that."

Ravenna made her way around Kalakuta and knelt near his back. He tried to roll over to keep her in sight, but she gently pushed his hip to keep him on his side. "Shh, dear, don't worry" she murmured. "Everything will be fine. You rest."

Softer now, as to a baby at the edge of sleep, she sang.

Come now my dear, hold me close, hold me near.
Kiss my lips and whisper rough oaths in my ear.
Dry my tears with hard love, and caresses severe.
Let our joining allay all our pain and our fear.

With the last fading note, Ravenna reached under the massive tail and gently slid the stone totem deep within the monster's anus.

Not knowing what to expect, failure, triumph, a final, violent tirade before death or a dangerous combustion of the abominable body, Knox gasped and was about to shout at the lady to run. Instead, he held his breath and watched.

Kalakuta turned to look the woman in the eye and trilled again his high-pitched purr of contentment. As he rolled back over he let out a long, quiet sigh as if relieved of a terrible burden, then slowly and silently faded away.

Three men and two women remained motionless and silent.

From high above in the makeshift press box, Tom snarled, "Well *that* was a big fucking letdown! No blood, no gore? No final showdown, blades going snicker-snack and bones going crackity-crack? No blinding light enveloping the beast as it screams and pulls apart at the sinews? *Just a fucking goodnight kiss?*"

Tim tisked. "Brother, you have a very big mean streak."

"Yeah? Well, you have a very small cock!"

Chapter 24 - Mixed Marriage and Metaphors

Ravenna stood and sighed, gazing down at the spot where Kalakuta, trusting her with his life, had met his end at her hand.

After another moment of stunned silence, Bilge breathed, "Here is a wonder if you talk of wonders!"

Squid whispered, "I wonder what it bodes?"

"Peace" said Knox, dropping his halberd. "It bodes a chance to live in peace."

Knox pushed through the jungle foliage and ran the length of the stone bridge, shouting, "Ravenna! My love, you've won!" He reached her at the center of the rock and captured her in his strong arms, planting a hungry kiss on her lips.

Ravenna cried out in shock at first, then melted and returned the rough embrace as the pirate freed her mouth and kissed her cheeks, forehead, and neck. She gasped and laughed with delight at his antics until he again took possession of her lips.

Bilge and Squid came out of hiding and stood together at the edge of the water, arms around shoulders, grinning at the happy couple.

Adelaide jogged heavily across the sand, waving her arms and crying out a litany of unrecognizable but clearly overjoyed shouts, whoops and chortles. As she circled the lagoon and approached the stone bridge, Squid and Bilge ran to her. The three elders embraced, laughing like children.

Ravenna melted in the pirate's arms as their kiss became languid and soft. When they parted, Knox whispered, "You saved us all, dear Ravenna. I was wrong about you, thinking you were just a weak-willed girl. You have the heart of a pirate, and I love you. Be mine, I beg you. Say you will be mine forever."

Ravenna felt his words flow through her body like liquid fire, suffusing every muscle with a warmth she'd longed for and feared she'd never find. Her eyes glistened into his under heavy lids, and her delicate lips turned upward in a slight smile. She felt Knox press himself against her, his body insistent and warm.

"Let's run off" he said, "find someplace to ourselves, and seal our union with our bodies, the way be both so desperately want."

Ravenna's knees weakened. She felt as though she could let herself fall and he would catch her, carry her away and give her everything she ever wanted. *He will marry me and...*

The word snapped her from the daydream like icy water on a candle flame. Her eyes widened. She gasped a breath and pushed at the pirate's chest, struggling against his strong hold.

"Ravenna? What is it?"

"Oz" she said, barely above a whisper, "my betrothed, my love, my Captain Oz. I am his, not yours."

"You can't mean that. He doesn't love you, not like I do. He can't give you what you want, what you *need*. I can! I *will*!"

"No." She pushed him again with more force, her face hardening into a scowl. "I must find him. I must go to him!"

Knox held her, his strength overpowering, his eyes now flickering with desire and anger. "Ravenna, please!"

Adelaide heard the lady's cries and broke away from the men, waddling quickly toward the couple. "Release her, varlet! Dog-hearted scut, I said let her go!"

Ravenna struggled and screamed, "Oz! Oh captain, my captain!"

The nun quickened her pace and drew the small dagger from her pocket. "Unhand the lady thou rank, plume-plucked, boar-pig thou! Swag-bellied ratsbane! Gut-griping bladder!"

"Ravenna, please!" cried the pirate, "please, you must be mine! I cannot live without you-yow-wow-ow-*ow*!"

Knox *yowed* in pain with each knife-jab the little nun poked into his haunch, but still held Ravenna by her wrists as she screamed for Oz and kicked at her captor's shins.

Squid and Bilge caught hold of the bloodthirsty Adelaide and pulled her away, still cursing and spitting at Knox. Squid managed to take her dagger, which deflated her rage. She slumped into the old salt's arms, panting her curses. He sat and held her while Bilge fanned his hands to give her air and patted her flushed and sweaty cheeks.

A sudden shout, "Knox!" stopped every movement and stilled every voice.

All watched as Captain Ozymandias Wembleye emerged from the sea, striding through the surf and onto the beach toward the lagoon.

"Release her, Knox, damn you, or I shall be... very... put out."

The pirate let go of Ravenna's arms and faced Oz. "So, the sea gods didn't take you, eh? Well then, I see I still have a duty to perform." He drew his sword but threw it away and took up his dagger. "Squid, give the captain your knife so we can fight fairly. I'll make quick work of... of..."

Knox's words trailed off as he and the others listened to a rising sound, a rushing and roaring beneath the surface of the water. It began offshore and moved toward them along the inlet to the lagoon, rising in pitch and intensity as the water churned and swirled. The roar and the bubbling, frothy water moved into the lagoon itself, until it surrounded the rock and splashed all there with the spray of its effervescence.

The three men and two women on the rock gathered at the center and stood back-to-back, a full circle defense against they knew not what creature or power that boiled the water from the shore to the lagoon.

The rushing sound and the churning foam in the lagoon ceased, replaced by a hundred mermen, merwomen and merchildren rising to the surface, faces and hair of every hue, smiling at the people cowering in the center, crooning a long, soft, single note of "ooooooommmmmmm." Beyond the lagoon, a thousand more of them crowded the shoreline, all smiling and singing, all attending the clutch of frightened people on the rock.

Oz walked the length of the stone bridge and smiled at the lady. He raised his hand and showed her a large, ancient key, then knelt and used it to free her ankle from the cruel cuff that held her captive.

When he stood, Ravenna let out a squeal of delight and threw her arms about his neck, kissing his mouth and cheeks, blubbering his name and wetting his face with her joyful tears. "Oh Oz, my darling! You're alive and well! I was sure the monster had killed you and... and..."

Her next words faded away as she watched a woman swim into the lagoon from the sea, a stunning, red-haired beauty who effortlessly swam closer, her eyes fixed on the captain, her smile radiant. All the other Merpeople parted to make way and bowed their heads as she passed. When she reached the rock, she bobbed in the water and held the captain's gaze with glistening, sultry eyes. Then, without effort, she launched herself onto the edge of the rock and sat, revealing her long, gray body and fluked tail, the pearly skin of her belly and chest and her large, firm breasts framed by the long tendrils of her deep red hair.

"Ozzz" she sang, still piercing him with her stare.

"Ozzz" echoed the others.

Hiding in their jungle press box, Tim and Tom nudged each other and winked.

"Shit's about to get real" Tom said.

"Indubitably" said Tim.

Knox, Adelaide, Bilge and Squid stood mesmerized by the sight, saying nothing.

Ravenna held Oz tight. "Who is *that?*"

Oz cleared his throat. "Darling, this is Eve, Queen of the Merfolk."

"Queen?"

"Eve? This is Lady Ravenna."

"Raaavennaaa" the queen sang in a rising melody, bowing her head in reverence.

Again, her subjects responded to her call. "Raaavennaaa."

"And how does she know *you*?" Ravenna's eyebrow cocked at Oz and her smile melted away.

"Captain Ozymandias Wembleye" said the queen, "has rescued me and my entire tribe from the monster Kalakuta, as I knew he would."

"As you *knew he would?*" Ravenna asked the queen. "Since when?"

"Since we met, this morning, when he made a solemn vow to save us."

"Wait a minute" Ravenna said, now breaking free from Oz's embrace. "You were with *her*, this morning?"

"Well, um, yes dear. You see—"

"Before I found you? At the lagoon?"

"Yes, just before, in fact, and—"

Eve languidly curled a long strand of her shining hair around one finger. "Yes, our beautiful moment together when we consummated our love and our promises to one another."

"Consummated?" gasped Ravenna, *"Consummated?"*

"Consummated?" said Bilge and Squid in unison.

"As in...?" Knox ventured.

Tim pretended to look at a pocket-watch in his hand. "Five, four, three, two, one..."

Tom pointed and shouted, "Cue the *Liar Revealed Trope!*"

"You *fucked a fish?*" Ravenna screamed.

"Not a *fish*, dear, more of a cetacean, you know, a sort of sea mamm—"

"She's a fish where it counts!"

"We are not fish" the queen said, now regarding Ravenna with the downcast glance of royalty. "We carry and bear our young within our bodies, as you do. And..." She gazed again at the captain with eyes of devotion, "I can already feel the new life that stirs within me, the fruit of our blessed union, my king."

"King?" blurted a befuddled Knox.

"That was rather quick" said the surprised captain.

"New life?" gasped an increasingly angry Adelaide.

"Are you sure?" asked an understandably curious Oz.

"Very sure" said the proud and obviously aroused queen.

"You *fathered* a *baby fish?*" shouted a now thoroughly disgusted Ravenna.

"Cockered, pottle-deep barnacle!" screamed the red-faced, snarling nun.

Ravenna cursed, "Die, fish fucker!" and pushed Oz into the lagoon.

Eve cried out, "My king!" and dove after him.

All of Eve's subjects submerged as well. For a moment, the only sounds were the waves lapping at the shore and a gentle breeze stirring the leaves and fronds of the jungle.

Exhausted, Ravenna fainted into the pirate's arms.

From deep within the waters of the lagoon, a deep rumbling sound arose and grew slowly louder, strong enough to shake the rock where the three men and two women stood, like an underwater volcano in the first seconds of eruption.

In their high redoubt, Tom pretended to move a chess piece and grinned. "Black queen to F2. Check, fish-fucker."

Tim studied the invisible board, then mimed a move. "White king to C1, queenside castle, my mean-spirited little brother."

"Little?"

"Oh, do please give it a rest."

Chapter 25 - On With the Show, This is It?

The ground-shaking rumble again moved the waters of the lagoon, stirring them clockwise, creating a vortex swirl. Speeding with every second, the waters flowed in a deepening gyre around the rock where the perplexed people stood and stared in wonder. Ravenna regained her senses and held tight to the pirate, watching through frightened eyes as the speed of the whirlpool increased and the roar grew louder.

Soon they could see that the cause of the speeding water was the Merfolk swimming around the rock, dozens of them, swimming below the surface with powerful beats of their tails, whipping the water into a frenzied, foaming orbit. The beating of their tails and a deep chord they all sang in unison combined into a thunderous reverberation, a chorus of perfect harmony that shook land and water alike.

Then, rising from the midst of the Merpeople, they watched as Oz slowly rose to the surface, carried along by Eve, swimming on her back and cradling the unconscious, naked man in her strong arms. Now the beat of the tails began to synchronize, the roar shifting to a rhythm, like that of a massive heart, a *thrum, thrum, thrum* that mated with the singular lyric note into a song of birth, of new life, the song sung by stars at the creation of the world.

Eyes closed and face peaceful, Oz lay on his back in the Mer Queen's arms like a man enjoying a pleasant nap as she sped him around the center rock, faster with every circle, her great tail splashing a high counterpoint to the *thrum, thrum, thrum* from the rhythmic swimming of her subjects. The oceanic heartbeat grew louder and the voiced note higher as their speed increased, the water now white with foam and spray.

Ravenna was first to notice and point. "Look! He's *changing*!"

Three men and two women watched in dumb fascination as the captain's legs fused together into one large mass of muscle. With a few more circuits his feet merged, flattened and spread out as a growing tail. Soon all his body below his navel that once made him a man transformed into a solid body of powerful muscle, the lower half of a dolphin like the others. His manhood elongated into a pointed tube that nestled within a tight slit on his underside. Finally, the pale pink skin darkened into gray flesh over a white underbelly.

The change completed, Eve sang a high-pitched warble that echoed over the shoreline. The swimmers signaled back with a counterpoint whistle and stopped the beating of their tails, the water now carrying them all in a slowing spiral around the rock.

Still laying within Eve's arms, Oz suddenly opened his eyes and smiled. Before the whirlpool had stopped, he turned over to drop himself into the water and began his own frenzied swim. The others swam to the edges of the lagoon and watched as he sped around and around, his new body strong and sleek, the undulations of his tail splashing out a tempo of sheer exuberance.

Then he dove and disappeared. The water slowed and lost its effervescence, the only sound the last ripples and a slight breeze in the trees.

This time, Knox was the first to see. "There!"

From deep below Oz rose and launched himself into the air, screaming his triumph in an earsplitting cry of utter joy. He reached his height, turned himself with expert skill and descended to cut into the water like an arrow, diving deep again with barely a splash.

The thousands of Merfolk offshore and the dozens within the lagoon screeched and laughed and cried out in delight. When Oz surfaced again, he shook water from his hair and smiled at the unrestrained welcome. Eve swam to him and wrapped her arms around his shoulders, capturing his mouth in a deep kiss while her subjects shouted in unison, *Oz! Oz! Oz!*

When they parted, they turned to face the sea, and Eve announced, "Behold! Oz, King of the Mers!"

The refrain from the elated people echoed across the island, "Behold! Oz, King of the Mers!"

"Behold! Oz!" the queen continued, "Defeater of Kalakuta!"

"Behold, Oz! Defeater of Kalakuta!"

Having regained her senses, Ravenna frowned. "Hey, wait a minute. I'm the one who killed Kalakuta."

Eve swam to the rock. "Yes, dear Ravenna, you did kill Kalakuta, and for that I and my people are eternally grateful. If you wish, we can make you a Merwoman, and you can live with us in bliss. And you may have blessed love with Oz too, for as King of the Mers he is the prime lover to all of us, and we share our loving and sex completely."

Huddled together with Bilge and Adelaide, Squid whispered, "It's *good* to be the king."

Though she laughed with the sailors, the little nun grumbled, "*Too* good, these rutting, fish fornicating flap-knackers."

"In fact" the queen said, looking to each of the people huddled together on the rock, "you could all join us, if you wish. Ours is a perfect paradise, and our lives are long and happy and incredibly, unbelievably passionate. All we do is sing and eat and drink and engage in innumerable sexual encounters in twosomes and threesomes and tensomes, or we just roil together in the sea in the hundreds until happily exhausted."

Ravenna looked to the former captain, bobbing in the water and grinning happily. "Is that the life you want, Oz."

"Well, dear, it's not so much a matter of *wanting*, as it is more of a *fait accompli*. I've sired a child with Eve and the Merfolk have made me their king, so it would be rude in the extreme to refuse their kind welcome. You understand, don't you dear?"

"I suppose."

"Another blessing is that I have never felt cleaner in my life. I am perpetually in the bath. It's a dream come true!"

"It's just that, is it?" asked the pirate, "and not all the fish fucking?"

"We're not fish, damn you, Knox."

"Well, fish or not, you still owe me for my dear Bonnie's life, Oz. But I can't very well duel you now, can I?"

"I'm afraid not. You would simply slaughter me on land, and I could easily drown you at sea. We're at a bit of an impasse."

Eve said, "Now that Kalakuta is no more, we have powerful magic. If you don't want to join us, ask for whatever you wish, and we will grant it."

"Anything?" Knox asked, eyebrows raised.

"Almost anything. We can't bring back your beloved from the dead. But anything else."

The pirate stroked his whiskered chin and thought for a moment. "What about a ship, then? A fast ship, with many cannon, and a crew to sail her? Can you do that?"

"If that is your wish, then yes" said the Mer Queen.

Knox looked at Ravenna. "What say you, lady? You could come with me, be my love, and sail the seas. Or, if you desire, I will take you home to Hudson. Otherwise" he pointed to Oz in the lagoon, "you can stay with the fish king here."

"Damn your soul, Knox! We are *not fish!*"

With a frown and furrowed brow, Ravenna looked from Knox, to Oz, to Eve, and back again. "These are not choices at all. Go with you, to be nothing but a helpmeet, a slave, always an afterthought as you fight and plunder and leave me to what? Cook and clean for you and relieve your urgings when you can't find maidens to rape?"

"No, dear, no! It would not be like that!"

"Or stay here and become like Oz, like them? Half one thing and half another, never all of either, living an idle life of boundless pleasure but no challenge?"

"I can assure you" said the Mer King, "that you would not be idle here. Did you see us swimming? The swimming is wonderful beyond belief."

"And after the swimming? And the eating and the drinking and the indiscriminate waterborne orgies?"

"Well. There's sleeping."

Ravenna sighed. "No thank you."

"Then home, my lady?" said the pirate. "I swear on my honor I will not touch you during the voyage. I will return you to your father and mother unharmed and unsullied. I will even forgo your ransom, so that you may go on living as you were before."

Ravenna let out an exhausted laugh. "The last of my terrible choices. Return to the life I had before? Before all this adventure and danger, overcoming terrible monsters and feeling the blessings of deep fear and high joy, the thrill of victory and the agony of defeat?" She gestured at Oz. "Go back to being a pampered princess waiting for the next foppish captain to come along and underwhelm me with his feigned affection and selfish vanity?"

Up in their treetop, the monkey brothers laughed.

Tom said, "Oooh, whatta burn!"

"He won't get the insult" said Tim.

"She pointed right at him!"

"Wager?"

"How much?"

"Loser goes to get fruit."

"You're on."

Oz said, "Oh, that won't happen, my love. I'm sure someone just as fine, brave, and well-groomed as myself will come along."

Tim hooked a thumb over his shoulder. "Make sure they're ripe."

"Asshole" said Tom and scampered off.

Ravenna shook her head. "No, those are no choices at all. Do what you will, Knox. I'll not be your mistress nor a member of your crew. I won't be a fish..."

Oz made to object, but Eve shushed him.

"... and I can't go back to be what I was before. There's nothing left for me in this world."

She sat on the edge of the rock, lowered her face into her hands and cried quietly.

"Imagine your ship, Knox" Eve said, "picture it clearly in your mind, just as you would have it. My people will make your wish come true."

Turning his now sad face away from Ravenna, he looked out toward the shoreline and closed his eyes. He remembered a galleon he once defeated in battle, so beautiful and swift that he wept as he watched it burn and sink. He fixed the image of it in his mind and said, "Ready."

"D'ye think it possible?" Squid said.

"If it is" said the nun, tapping her knees and nipples and forehead to invoke her saint's protection, "then my faith in God and Saint Salacious will be shaken for sure."

Squid reached out and took the nun's hand. "Have faith in this, pet."

Adelaide smiled at the old salt.

Bilge took her other hand. "If your faith has room for one more?"

She squeezed the trusty sailor's hand. A teardrop rolled down her cheek.

Tom returned and handed a large ripe fruit to Tim, who took a bite and nodded in approval. "Excellent choice, dear brother."

"Live ta serve ya, wanker" said Tom. He sat and took a large bite of his own, chewed and swallowed. "So, what's happening?"

"Well, they seem to be setting up for the denouement, but I think it's a false ending."

"What makes you think that?"

Tim pointed to the lagoon. Eve was talking in whispers with Ravenna, their heads close and their speech animated. Ravenna nodded and smiled. Eve reached out and held the lady's hand in both of hers.

Tom nodded and stroked his feathery sideburns. "Uh, huh. Breaking the Rule of Three?"

"Precisely."

"Well then" Tom said, leaning back against a branch and waving his hand like a conductor with a baton, "on with the show."

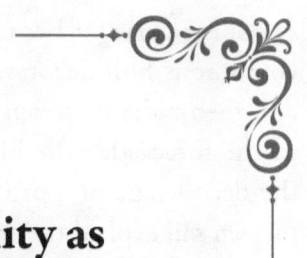

Chapter 26 - Reality as Magic, and Vice Versa

Standing with his eyes closed, Knox felt a shiver of embarrassment between his shoulders. The silence was total, save for the breeze and the lapping of waves, giving the pirate time to think himself foolish.

An entire ship? From thin air? Come on, Knox old man, be reasonable.

He remembered the magic he'd seen on this strange island — the bubbling stream appearing when most needed, the jade phallus killing Kalakuta, Oz transformed into a Merman, and made a king no less! Even the blasted talking monkeys were wonders not found in the world from which he came.

If these strange creatures can manifest a ship for me, I can live. If they cannot, I'm doomed. Stuck here, I won't become one of them. Ravenna won't have me. I'll never sail again. I'll surely die.

He opened his eyes. Hundreds of the Merfolk swam languidly in the shallow waves just beyond the strand, all eyes on him, faces bright with smiles.

They're waiting for me. What have I got to lose?

He closed his eyes and clasped his hands at his breastbone, calling up the memory of the beautiful galleon. If his thoughts and wishes were to give the Merpeople the blueprint, he would make the best of it.

How his heart leapt in his chest when he first spied it that bright day through his scope! Still far off, near the horizon, the elegant swooping curve of her outline stood stark against the bright sky, her voluptuous hull decorated a glistening black at the lower wale, then red, then radiant golden at the deck railing all the way from the stern to the forecastle. The billowing sails of her two main masts formed the décolletage of a proud, full breasted, high-born woman, and her mizzen sail evoked the train of a lady's headdress. She cut through the water like a knife and quickly tacked port and starboard to catch the slightest shift in wind.

That day, he lusted for the treasure in her hold more than the beauty herself, and later ached at the memory of sinking her after victory. But now he held only to the memories from before he ordered the first shot, when she gleamed in the sunlight and teased him with her beauty and agility.

The Merpeople in the waves closed their eyes and turned their faces to the sun, as if hearing the pirate's thoughts through the wind in their hair and the warmth on their skin. Then a low note sounded quietly in every throat, rising in volume, slowly growing into a sonorous blend as some voices rose to a major third, others to the fifth, the intervals harmonizing into a celestial trichord that touched the flesh of each living creature in the sea and on the land, vibrating the very corpuscles in their veins.

The chord grew louder as the people began swimming in circles — one small group forming a center by swimming clockwise, more encircling the first in counterclockwise motion, then a clockwise third, and a countering fourth. The circles multiplied and sped faster, tightening on each other as they created a frenzied whirlpool in the shallow waters.

Knox could wait no longer and opened his eyes, gasping at the sight. The whirling water rose into the air, the small center first, then the others in turn, circling and cascading into a frothing peak some two dozen feet high. But his smile turned dark as the growth slowed, the waters lost some ferment and the song dimmed in volume.

They need my dream!

The pirate captain fell to his knees in the sand, head down and eyes closed, hands folded in fervent prayer. He forced his thoughts back to that magnificent boat, how sprightly and proud she moved and how she glistened in the midday sun.

His reward came in the growing roar of the celestial harmony and the hiss of the ebullient waters stirred by the swift swimmers.

As he gave himself over to his inner vision, the sailors and the nun watched the mountain of water rise ever higher, spin ever faster, and the voices sing impossibly louder, until the reverberations shook rock and tree and bone.

When the base of the watery mountain grew to over a hundred feet across and the peak as high as a mainmast, Bilge pointed and whispered, "Look! It comes!"

At the waterline they saw the first solid shapes, the keel and low hull of the ship forming from slats of solid wood, locking together from the pointed prow to the wide stern, painted glossy black. Up and up the apparition took solid form, board after board of the hull stacking on the others below, turning red as they formed the mid decks, then gold as the ship grew higher.

The massive whirling cone of waters grew on, forming the great masts and rigging, the sails billowing and pennants fluttering on running lines. A row of cannon ports appeared midships, opening to reveal heavy guns. Lighter cannon appeared on the quarter deck and forecastle while the mizzen mast unfurled a great triangular sail and the long booms at the prow sprouted the sharp-angled jib canvas.

As each lower section finished, the water cleared and moved upward, revealing the completed work as solid and real as anything formed by the hands of men. The circling, swirling cone of foam rose higher, creating the upper sections of the ship as the lower shone glistening in the sun.

At last, the spinning mist shrank away to nothing as it reached the final height of the main mast. From its disappearing gyre appeared the crow's nest, then a great, black banner flying from the highest rigging, the center emblazoned with a pirate's crest: a bloody dagger driven through a laughing skull from crown to jaw.

The last of the waters dissipated, the hissing ceased, and the singing stilled.

Gasps from Adelaide, Squid, and Bilge pulled Knox from his dream. He lifted his face and stared at the sight, the ship before him an exact copy of the one he coveted and destroyed. He and the rest watched as the smiling Merfolk surrounding the boat cheered and waved in exultation.

Knox joined the men and Adelaide in breathless cries of wonder as they watched pirate sailors, dozens of them, appear on the deck from below and take up the tasks of preparation for a voyage. Clad in the typical garb of the criminal seaman — striped trousers, tall boots, billowy white shirts and red bandannas — they made their way onto deck of the ship, fanning out to the stern and prow. Working the rigging and shouting oaths, they broke into sailor songs full of vulgar sentiments and off-key harmonies.

Still unsure if he was dreaming, Knox turned to face Oz and Eve, laying in each other's arms on the black rock of the lagoon, smiling.

"I can never understand, let alone repay, the kindness you show me today. If that ship is real, then you have performed a miracle worthy of a saint, but you offer the gift to an undeserving scoundrel with more blood on his hands than waters of the seas."

"The ship is real" said the Mer Queen, "and it is yours with our blessings and our love. You and your friends saved my people—" she stopped, smiled at Oz and said "— *our people*, from oblivion. For that, you are most deserving of all we can offer."

"You *are* a scoundrel, Knox" Oz said, smiling at the pirate, "but then so am I, and see the gifts bestowed on me? Let's go our ways and wish each other well. What say you?"

Knox grinned. "Aye, we are both scoundrels, Oz, and worse than that. You know, do you not, that I intend to use that magnificent vessel to ply my trade again, a buccaneer ready to take on the best ships of the merchant classes, plundering their wealth without mercy or remorse?"

"I do."

The pirate's smile slanted a bit, and he winked an eye at the captain. "I have come to think that such a life lived only for myself is neither honorable, nor satisfying. So, I vow to you and the queen this day, that I will plunder the wealthy, as I 've always done, and give the booty away to those in the world from whom much of that wealth has been stolen."

At the wide-eyed stare from Oz, Knox raised a hand and laughed. "Oh, I'll have my share. But how much gold can I spend, how much meat can I eat, how much wine can I drink? The rest will go to those most needy, and more deserving than I. With this, maybe I can reconcile the sinner and the saint in my heart and bring good into the world, to balance the books."

"Perhaps you can, Knox." Oz saluted. "Fair winds, captain."

Knox bowed deeply. "Long life and joy to you, great king and queen."

When he rose, he turned to look in every direction. "Where's Ravenna? If she won't go with me, I want to say farewell."

Eve said, "The lady has gone off to find her own way. You should go now to find yours."

His smile and bright eyes faded. He turned toward the boat again and faced Squid, Adelaide and Bilge, standing in his way with expectant faces.

"If ye please, cap'n" said the old salt, "we three would be honored to sign on for your next voyage."

"If you'll have us *all*" said Bilge, "we find ourselves bound together by shared adventure and spirit."

Knox looked to Adelaide. "Is that what binds you together with these men, dear little nun? Adventure and spirit?"

"What's it to you, thou fobbing codpiece? We want to join your quest for the poor and downtrodden peoples, and whatever force pulls us to your orbit is for you to thank God and not for you to question, thou whoreson, beetle-headed, flap-eared knave!"

Tim and Tom watched from their high nest, both overstuffed with fruit, lethargic in the hot sun. "I tell you" Tom said, "I hate human beings with a purple passion. But of all I've seen, I like that woman. She has more than spunk. She has the best cursing vocabulary of any living creature, including me."

"Agreed" said Tim. "I'll miss them, truth be told. And her most of all."

"Yeah. I'll miss them too. Fuck me if I understand *that*."

"Maybe they will come back to visit sometime."

"Hmm, yes, I suppose they could." The vulgar brother stared at the great ship for a moment. His smile grew bright under narrowed eyes that bespoke wicked thoughts.

"Tom?"

"Don't bug me. I'm thinking."

Knox led his new band toward the water's edge as the crew aboard the ship lowered a launch skiff and rowed for shore.

Oz whispered to Eve, "Tell me, that is a real ship, yes? I've never been a magical being before. Will it hold together, or disappear like a fog when they are at sea?"

"It is real, my king. All reality is magic, is brought into being by magic, held together by magic, transformed by magic. Some just understand the workings better than others. You will enjoy learning, trust me."

"I trust you entirely, my queen."

They embraced, kissed, and fell into the water.

Chapter 27 - Pas de Deux
for Captains

Knox was first to board the ship, stepping lightly and carefully on the main deck until he felt solid wood under his boot and not some illusion made of water and vain hope.

The crew of newly-made-human pirates swarmed their captain, cheering and whistling and calling out his name. When Bilge and Squid helped Adelaide aboard, the men fell quiet and bowed to her, then saluted the two elder seamen.

"Quite the welcome" Knox said. He smiled at the sensation of the boat rocking under his feet, a feeling of homecoming.

One of the crew, a living, breathing cliché of a pirate with a red bandanna on his head, a huge gold hoop earring and an eye patch, stepped forward. "Beggin' the captain's pardon, but she's ready ta sail, an' the boys are all itchin' fer a fight, waitin' only on yer orders, sir."

Knox was about to give the order when he stopped and looked back to shore. Eve and Oz and a score of Merfolk were bobbing in the water of the lagoon, smiling and waving. He scanned the beach up and down but saw no sign of Ravenna. When he glanced at Adelaide, then Squid and Bilge, he saw his own sadness reflected in their faces. With closed eyes he nodded at the thought he dared not speak; *She is not coming.*

He shook himself to dispel the chill in his spine and gave the pirate a hearty clap on the shoulder. "Very well, uh, what's your name, sailor?"

"Whelk, sir."

"Whelk, you will be my boatswain. Obey these three" he pointed to Adelaide and her escort, "as my first mates. Standby to make sail!"

"Aye, aye, sir. An' where to, cap'n?"

Knox looked out over the prow toward the setting sun, then aft at the gathering twilight. He turned back, his face lit reddish in the dying light, and pointed. "That way. We will sail beyond the sunset."

An hour later, sheets billowing with a steady tail wind, the ship cut frothing wake in a sea flat as glass. Knox walked the entire ship from the ballast hold to the bowsprit to learn her every secret. Now he stood on the quarterdeck looking out over his crew as they busily handled sail and line, singing songs that called for a fight and promised no mercy to whatever vessel crossed their path.

Lost in thought about the love he left behind, he could not enjoy the bracing wind and the rhythmic rocking as he always did when setting out on a new adventure.

The three first mates made their way up to the deck to join him, ending his internal monologue of woe.

Bilge said, "Eve and her people certainly did right by us. Everything is ship-shape and we're fully provisioned. The ship's cook has great slabs of beef roasting and pies baking, and the wine kegs are full to bursting!"

"And the treasure!" said the old salt. "Did ye see, cap'n? Half the hold is full ta the rafters with gold and jewels, enough to satisfy a king!"

Knox smiled at his companions. "Aye, I saw. We'll take enough for ourselves to live on, then give the rest away to some needful worthies before we go spoiling for a fight."

"I'll look after accounting for the booty" said the little nun. "You'll not be taking more than your fair share. You will give the rest to the poor and downtrodden peoples, or you'll have my boot in yer arse, thou fobbing, fat-kidneyed fustilarin."

Laughing with the men, Knox said, "You've got a deal, dear lady. You shall be the conscience of our ship in matters spiritual and financial."

When their laughter faded, the three men and the woman stood at the railing for a while, staring out over the prow of the ship.

A sudden, shrill whistle broke the quiet.

"Knox Bloodworthe!" a woman screamed from somewhere high above, "you cowardly bastard!"

Knox and the others searched the rigging for the source of the curses.

"How dare you make yourself bold to give orders on *my ship?*"

Knox caught sight of her first. She stood on the top spar of the mizzen mast, a rigging line in one hand, the other on her hip. Her long, billowing gown of red silk and brace of black petticoats waved in the breeze, the laces of her tight bodice straining to keep her full breasts from escape. A rapier, dagger, and pistol adorned her wide, gold buckled belt, and on her head at a jaunty angle sat a large tricorne of red with black feathers. Her long, thick, flaxen hair was black and shiny as a polished onyx gemstone.

"Ravenna?" he called out.

"Salacious, preserve us" gasped the nun.

"A beauty to behold" whispered Bilge.

"A pirate's wet dream" said Squid, taking a half-hearted slap to his cheek from Adelaide.

The deck hands left off their tasks and gathered near the mizzenmast, craning their necks to see this new wonder.

The woman suddenly leapt from her perch, took hold of a long rigging line and slid down to the lower spar of the mizzenmast, where she wrapped her arms and legs around another line and rode it down to the railing. Leaping to the deck, she faced Knox, drew her rapier and pointed it at the pirate's eyes.

"On your guard, lowlife scum! Try to steal my ship, will you? I'll chop you into shark bait before I'll surrender her."

The men, crowded on the main deck below, let out a roar of cheers and whistles.

Mouth still gaping in surprise, Knox repeated, "Ravenna?"

"Ravenna is dead. I am Lady Raven, Siren of the Seaways, and this is my ship!"

The sailors let out a resounding, "Huzzah!"

"Your ship?"

"Yes, now surrender and you may live as a member of my crew. Refuse and die where you stand."

From the growing crowd, a low and poignant, "Ooooo!"

Knox's dark face split into a broad, white smile. "Ravenna, darling, you came to join me after all. My love!" He rushed toward her with his arms outstretched, but the sword did not dip, and he stopped just before losing an eye.

From below, a quiet but unified gasp, "Whoa!"

He held his arms up in surrender, but still smiled. "Darling, you can't be serious. I'm overjoyed you are here, but you can't be a ship's captain."

She grinned. "Correction. I already own this ship and command it. And I call myself Raven, so address me as such. I've left that other life behind."

"Very well, Lady Raven. But you can't really mean to take over this ship."

She leaned forward just enough to press the sharp point of the sword against the hollow at the base of the pirate's throat. He grimaced but did not back away.

The sailors hissed in sympathetic discomfort.

Her voice low and cool, she said, "Did you not promise me anything - *anything* - for saving you from Kalakuta?"

"Well, uh, yes, but that was—"

"That" she said, jabbing his flesh and making him wince, "was a promise. And you'll keep your promise, or you will die."

Knox tried to push her sword away, but she flicked it out of his reach then quickly back, stabbing his shoulder and drawing blood. He cried out at the pain and clutched the wound. The wide-eyed look of surprise on his face melted into a teeth-baring grimace and flickers of anger ignited in his pupils.

Two of the sailors started taking bets on the winner. Another offered odds on the number of wounds.

"Well?" she said, grinning. "What will it be, then? Surrender or death?"

Knox stepped back and drew his sword. "I'll not surrender, and I'll not die, but I will teach you a lesson about who owns this ship. Defend yourself!"

With a growl in his throat, Knox lunged at Raven, who retreated coolly and parried his first and second thrusts, then held ground on the third, parried and delivered a riposte to his sword arm that slashed his sleeve and drew a crimson line in his flesh. She counterattacked immediately, pushing the pirate back on his heels with vicious cutting swipes, until he pivoted to let her pass and fell back to regain his stance.

Astonished, Knox glanced at her feet, completely hidden under the skirt and petticoats of her gown. He'd always relied on reading his enemy's stance and footwork and felt the disadvantage keenly when Raven charged with a flurry of cuts and thrusts. He barely beat her blade away each time, attempting a counter that opened him up and earned him another shallow slash across his chest.

Holding at a distance, Knox panting, Raven smiled. "Yield, Knox? You will hold high rank and honor on my ship if you do."

"You've been bewitched" Knox gasped. "Eve gave you magic to best me with a blade!"

Raven glanced at Adelaide, beaming a joyous smile at her, flanked by the two men with gape-mouthed shock on their frozen faces.

"Us girls have to stick together." She winked at the little nun, who gave out a whooping shout.

The men echoed her cheer then barked in unison, "Girls! Girls! Girls!"

She faced Knox again. "I'm not invincible. If you won't surrender, then defeat me. If you can, the ship is yours. But if I win..." She let her voice trail off and flicked the tip of her sword twice in invitation.

The bet takers below began offering double or nothing.

The pirate gathered himself up like a bull ready to charge, then ran full speed at her, slashing wildly. The sheer force of his attack pushed her back to the edge of the deck, almost sending her overboard into the sea. She braced her leg against the railing and struggled under the onslaught. Knox pressed the advantage with a fusillade of thrusts but could not get past her defense. Desperate to escape the close fight, Raven grabbed hold of his blade's forte near the guard with her off hand and slammed his nose with her pommel.

Knox staggered backward, holding his now freely bleeding nose, gasping for breath and moaning curses.

Half the sailors below cheered. The rest groaned in anticipation of losing their wagers.

The lady circled her quarry slowly, at the ready, watching as he managed to recover both his eyesight and his resolve. Once behind him, she whispered, "Last chance, Knox."

Without turning, he growled, "Last chance for you!" then whirled and swept his sword back and forth at her, not aiming, long past his ability to strategize or control his rage.

Raven anticipated his fury and backed away, letting him waste his strength on useless slashes, waiting for him to return to a thrusting attack. When he did, she stepped in and pivoted on her toes until she met him shoulder to shoulder. Before he could react she caught the guards of his hilt with her quillon and swept the sword from his hand. It flew across the deck and landed with a clang against the wood frame of the great skylight.

The lady pirate spun again and faced her defeated foe, blade aimed at his heart.

Exhausted, Knox fell to his knees and bowed his head.

The clamor of men's voices rose on the main deck as the sailors cheered their winnings and moaned their losses, the bookmakers all grinning with greed at their inevitable profits.

"Kill me quickly" Knox groaned. "If I can't be captain then I am nothing. I ask now only the mercy of a swift death."

"You are not nothing, Knox Bloodworthe." Raven walked slowly around the defeated pirate as she spoke. "You are a treasure, a rare and beautiful example of a man with strength, and wit, and passion and skill. I would as soon toss a chest of treasure into the depths as destroy a man like yourself."

The three first mates looked on in silence, unbreathing. The sailors below fell silent.

When she stood behind the kneeling man, she shrugged. "But, since you still need to learn the lesson of who rules this ship…"

Her voice faded off as she swept her arm and dealt the back of the pirate's head a vicious blow with the hilt of her sword. He slumped forward on the deck and heaved a long sigh.

The men below cheered and whistled and took up the chant, "Ra-ven! Ra-ven! Ra-ven!"

She pointed to Bilge and Squid. "Take him to the captain's quarters."

The two men hesitated until Adelaide shouted, "You heard her, did ye not, ye clay-brained clotpoles? Move yer arses!"

They hustled to Knox and took his limp body by the arms, dragging him toward the ladder leading to the main deck.

Raven ran to Adelaide and whispered. "Quickly, bring bandages and wine, food, and a coil of stout rope.

"Rope, m'lady?"

"I still have a wild stallion to break."

Chapter 28 - Now and Forever

Deep, throbbing pain was all Knox knew as his soul rose from blackness toward the light.

He groaned, eyes still closed, heartbeats pounding between his temples like a vengeful blacksmith with hammer and anvil. All the world shrank to only the agony in his head. He groaned again, the sound and the feel of the air in his throat spurring him to wake further, pain be damned.

He could now feel his body, more at ease than miserable, warm and resting on softness. Flickering light danced through his closed eyelids, and the scent of roasted meat teased his aching and swollen nose. The pang of hunger it sparked reached him through all his afflictions.

The craving for food spurred him to move his stiff and sore limbs, but he could not bend or stretch them. He opened his eyes and lifted his head to confirm the worst; he'd been bound at the wrists and ankles to the four posts of a large bed with strong, thick hemp rope. He was stark naked.

"Awake now, are you darling?"

Lady Raven, Siren of the Seaways, sat on a simple wooden chair next to the bed, one booted foot on the side rail, sipping wine from a jeweled cup. She'd pulled her skirts up to reveal her shapely leg to the thigh, leaning back with a smug smile on her face and her ornate tricorne tilted back on her head.

Her lovely face, pale and blushed and framed by her long, jet-black tresses, washed away all the pirate's torment for a few blessed moments.

"Care for some wine, dear?"

She moved slowly and deliberately from the chair, eyes locked with his, placing her bare knee on the mattress and leaning forward. Knox could not help glancing at her bosom as she approached, and she laughed quietly at his boyishness.

She held out her goblet. "Have some of mine. It's very good."

He struggled to keep his head lifted as she placed the cup to his lips. The first taste set his thirst on edge. He gulped greedily, a tiny rivulet of the deep red liquid running down his cheek.

She lifted the cup. "There, that's better, isn't it? Oh, but you spilled." Leaning down again, she gently licked the dribbled wine from his cheek, then gave his lips the lightest of kisses.

Her beauty, her touch, her scent, his memory of her passionate embrace, made Knox forget his predicament for a handful of heartbeats. When he tried to reach out to her, again finding himself imprisoned by the taut ropes, he yanked against the restraints with all his strength. Raven stood and watched, smiling, as he fought for freedom and failed.

He gave up the struggle and shouted, "What in the devil's name are you doing, woman?"

"Testing your loyalty, captain."

"Captain? Why call me that? You said you are captain of this ship."

"No. I said I own and command this ship. I make all the decisions. Where to go and when, who to fight, who to help, what to buy, what to sell, what to steal. Consider me an admiral, or perhaps commodore. But it's true I am no sailor. So, I need a captain. If you will swear your loyalty, and keep your word, that can be you."

Knox held his breath, then burst out laughing. "By the sea gods, what foolishness! The men can't serve under two captains, no matter what you call yourself. There can be only one!"

"You're the fool, Knox. You said yourself a pirate lives within us all. Mine is no longer hidden. I am Lady Raven, and I long to slit a throat and taste the blood from my blade!"

With the word, she drew the dagger from her belt and leapt on the bed, knee to the pirate's chest, the razor-edged blade against his throat.

Knox grunted as he bore her weight, then froze, feeling the cold steel a mere flick of her wrist away from opening his jugular.

"Together..." she breathed, her eyes wild and alive with lust for murder or sex or both, "together we would be invincible!"

Knox weighed his words before speaking. "And if I refuse? Will you kill me? Or make me some lowly swabbie, emptying honey buckets and manning the bilge pump?"

She laughed and stood again. "No, I would not. I meant what I said. You are a rare, beautiful, strong and intelligent man, a treasure. I would not rob the world of you. I want you for my own, to fight side by side and then fuck until our strength gives out." She stepped to the nearby captain's table and laid her dagger there. When she turned, she began unlacing her bodice.

"If you refuse me, I will disembark at the first port we find. You will take this ship, the one you promised to me when I held your life in my hands, and you can go to hell on it."

She opened her bodice and let it drop. Her nipples stood high and dark under the white cotton of the chemise.

"I will find my own ship, my own crew, and a captain I'll pay in gold instead of love. Then I will hunt you down and kill you. Or you will kill me." She smiled as she released the drawstring and dropped her skirt, then slowly, one by one, let her petticoats fall to the floor. "The choice is that simple, that stark, and the choice is yours."

Knox watched, wide-eyed, as she unlaced the chemise and let it slide down her shoulders and waist and legs until she stood pale and naked in the flickering, yellow candlelight, wearing only her tall, high-heeled jackboots and her feathered tricorne.

"Shall I leave my hat on?" she teased.

He watched wordlessly as she strolled closer, hands stroking softly from her thighs up and over the sleek, black hair of her mons, to her belly and on to her full, taut breasts. She pinched her nipples and jumped at the flash of pain, her smile now wicked and her eyes languid.

The sight pierced the pirate's belly and lit a flame. The warmth diffused lower. He felt the first twinge as his cock swelled and his balls tightened in anticipation.

She let out a guttural laugh and leapt on the bed, pinned the pirate's trapped arms with her knees and took hold of his dreadlocks with both hands.

"I rule, Knox. I command this vessel. I command *you!*"

Smothered in her sex, Knox could give no answer. She dripped wet with the honey of her desire, laying her weight against him, forcing his mouth into the opened, pulsing folds. She thrust her hips and pulled his hair to grind herself into his mouth, his nose, his chin then back again.

She growled like a cat in heat. "Drink me, you bastard! Suck and tongue me 'til I drown you! Drink!"

Knox gulped and swallowed, heart pounding with sparked lust and gasping for breath when she gave him the slightest respite. She threw her head back, the hat falling to the bed, grunting with every fevered thrust of her hips. He stretched his tongue as deep as he could, slurping and slobbering, then wrapped his lips around her swollen nub and sucked like it held the antidote to all pain. She let out a high-pitched squeal, shuddered, and flooded his face with a fresh wave of her essence.

Despite everything, his wounds and his anger and his near suffocation, he was transported by animal desire, his cock now hard and standing tall.

Sensing his rut, Raven turned and saw the object of her utmost greed. She gasped and pushed herself up from his face, scrambling lower until her hips hovered over his pillar. Without ceremony she sat and impaled herself to his balls, eyes rolled back to the whites, until the ridged head of his long, fat phallus rammed against her womb.

Her scream of release shook the timbers of the ship. She sat him deep and hard and gushed wave after wave of her slick juice over his thighs. When her lungs emptied, she drew a deep and ragged breath, then hammered his muscled chest with her fists as she lifted and sat him again and again. Her lithe body bucked and shivered with the agony of her highest pleasure until she slowed and panted and collapsed onto him, whimpering.

Listening outside the door, Squid and Bilge held Adelaide between them, all three breathless.

The little nun struggled a moment for air, then whispered, "Well, lads? Shall we see what amenities await us in *our* cabin?

Grinning and giggling like naughty children, the three first mates scampered away.

Still pinioned, Knox desperately wanted to hold the gasping woman in his arms but contented himself with kissing her hair. The pulsing of her fading climax worked his shaft, keeping him hard and ready.

The perfect key opened the lock of pain and regret that held him captive. Knox let his heart open, and his pride fall. "You rule" he said quietly, his deep voice reverberating through his chest into Raven's ear. "This ship is yours, and I am yours to command. I swear to you all my loyalty until the day I die."

She roused and slowly pushed herself up by his broad shoulders to meet his gaze. Her eyes glistened with tears of joy while her lips lifted into a wicked grin of still unsatisfied hunger.

"Now" she breathed, "we come to the final test."

Lifting her hips released her quim's hold on his manhood, still upright. She ran to the table and took up her dagger. Walking slowly to the bed, she held the blade aimed at his blood-engorged member.

He stared at her with fear-widened eyes. "Wha... what test?"

"You must prove that you are the Knox Bloodworthe of legend. The murderous, pitiless, bloodthirsty, *rapacious* Scourge of the Seaways."

The thin blade cut through the rope holding his left foot. She stepped around the bed to his right. "Out there, with the crew, and in all ways pertaining to this ship, I am in full command. Yes?" She pointed the dagger at his right foot.

"Yes, my love. You are in command."

She freed his right foot and moved on toward his hand. "But in here, alone in our cabin, in the secret chambers of our hearts, it is the pirate king who must rule. And to rule..." She pointed the blade to his right hand, "... a king must *take* what he desires. Is that not the way of the sea?"

Catching her meaning, Knox smiled. "Yes, my love, that is the way."

She cut the rope at his right hand then ran quickly to the other side of the bed, where his left wrist was still bound. He watched as she slowly laid the edge of the blade against the strands of hemp.

"Then hear me, Knox. When I free you I am the quarry and you the hunter. Try your best, for I will fight you with all I have. I will kill you if I can. If you are the man I hope you are, you will prevail, and I will have the pirate king I desire and deserve."

A flick of her wrist cut the rope. She ran to the far side of the large, round table and crouched, the dagger in her hand pointed at Knox's heart, promising death.

He rose slowly, his head nearly touching the low ceiling, and flexed his sore limbs. Raven flipped the dagger and caught it fighting style, blade below the fist, her eyes fixed on his still hard cock, smiling.

He strolled toward her, around one side of the table. She scurried opposite. He reversed direction and lunged. She did the same. They encircled the table again and once more before Knox sighed.

"No more games."

He launched himself over the table and captured her in his massive arms. They tumbled together to the floor, Raven screaming a war cry. She sank the dagger's tip into his shoulder once, then again. The pain spurred him to ruthless action. He released her arms and took hold of her weaponed hand, twisting the wrist without mercy and rolling her to her belly as he pinned her arm behind.

Her screams transformed from rage to agony.

With a swift move he wrenched the dagger from her grip and threw it away. Keeping her arm captive he clambered to his feet, dragging her with him. Once standing, he filled his free hand with her thick, black hair and slammed her, face first, onto the table.

The blow took her breath and stunned her thoughts. Standing over her and keeping her arm captive, he growled. "I *am* Knox Bloodworthe, wench, and I take what I want. Is this what *you* want?"

With each word she pounded the table with her free hand and gasped, "Yes, yes, yes!"

He took hold of both wrists. Gripping them in one hand behind her back, like reins to a horse. Kicking at her legs to spread them, he pressed the head of his cock against her open, dripping lips.

"In this room" he growled, panting with lust, "in our hearts, you are mine and I rule you."

"Yes."

"Say it!"

"You rule me, oh god, Knox, you rule me. Please, fuck me 'til I cry!"

He thrust himself into her fast and fully, and once to the hilt he pushed again, his muscled thighs and haunches taut as steel cables and glistening brown in the flickering candlelight. She screamed again, long, loud, and plaintive, like a dying lamb. Her every sinew convulsed as her sex gushed, her slickness pouring to the floor like a waterfall.

His pounding began, slowly at first, then faster, but always from crown to root, each merciless thrust making her grunt and gasp for breath. Soon he was the one lost to the agony of his bliss as he snarled and fucked her faster, her flesh rippling from haunches to breasts with each hit, echoes of his power.

The moment arrived. She felt the change.

"Come!" she screamed. "Fill me! Knox, my love, my captain! Fill me!"

He freed her arms, clutched her hips and pounded her with all his strength. Head back, he bellowed a lion's roar as his cock pulsed and pumped great jets of cum into her. She overflowed with his thick spunk and her glistening honey. Still he plunged in and out, slowing but not easing, shaking her womb with each thudding strike, until she wailed her surrender and cried, wetting the table with her tears and heaving ragged groans mixed with a demon's laughter.

When he finally stopped, still hard and deep, he leaned over to gently free her face from her thick hair and kissed her cheek.

"We own each other, my pirate queen" he breathed into her ear, "now and forever."

"Yes, my king" she sobbed. "Now and forever."

Chapter 29 - To Glory or Death

A bright, full moon hung low over the stern of the galleon and lighted the boat's way over the waveless sea.

With the mainsails luffed to spill wind she cruised at a leisurely pace, like a lady out for a stroll in the park. The gentle flapping of the loose canvas sounded out a quiet tattoo, as if a drum corps marched far away over a hill. The sailors on deck for the night watch attended to their tasks quietly, humming shanties under their breath, while those below caroused loudly and lewdly, their songs and wicked laughter spilling from the cannon ports and rising in the night air like invisible steam.

Knox and Raven leaned against the high railing at the stern, her wrapped in a blanket and the pirate's strong arms, the ship's lantern above them casting a soft golden glow over their shoulders. They stared out to sea for many minutes in silence. Her head rested on his chest while he pressed his face to her temple and breathed the perfume of her hair, needing no words to say what their bodies shared in caress and kiss and the thrum of heartbeats echoed between flesh pressed in tight embrace.

"My king?" she finally whispered.

"Yes, my queen?"

"Our ship needs a name. A good, strong name."

"Aye lady. She does."

"What would you name her?"

He leaned down to kiss her cheek. "I've don't know. What about *Ravenwing?*"

She laughed softly. "You are sweet, and you are always welcome to pander to my vanity. But no."

"Very well. Let's call her *Eve*, after the queen of the Merfolk who made her."

"That would be the honorable thing to do. But I am not honorable."

He laughed. "No, my queen. Neither am I."

"It must be something meaningful. Something that proclaims our cause, our purpose."

He shrugged. "I'm out of ideas, love. Have you a choice?"

"I have."

"Yes?"

"We should call her *The Bonnie Bones*."

She felt him stiffen and hold his breath. He waited a moment before asking, "Why?"

"For one thing, you will always love Bonnie. I saw it on your face when you spoke of her. Your love for her will always—"

"But, dear one—"

"Don't interrupt me. There's no need to protest. I know you are mine just as I am yours, now and forever. But she was precious to you, and you should honor her memory, and always remember your days and nights together with tenderness and joy."

He sighed. "You continue to amaze me, darling."

Through a smug grin she said, "And I always will."

Their laughter blended in the night air and fanned the flame of the lantern to burn brighter.

Raven turned to Knox and gazed into his eyes with a face that had lost its laughter. "But also, you must never forget what they did to her, the terrible, immoral cruelty. What my father did to her, and how he and his ilk callously take lives and fortunes and hope away from people like her, enriching themselves at the expense of the helpless."

She saw the pirate's face darken with his anger.

"We will be her revenge. And the revenge for all those made fodder for war and commerce, given no mercy, shown no quarter, starved and shackled and sheared of their very flesh by the moneyed parasites who sit on sacks of gold and call themselves royal."

His scowl lifted and morphed into a gleeful mask of dark joy as he stared out toward the invisible horizon of their fate. "Yes. *Yes*. She shall be *The Bonnie Bones*, and her name will stop the hearts of the wicked who hear it. Her sails on the horizon will turn the liver of every sailor sent to face her. They will run from her if they are wise or stand against her and be cut down like wheat. She will exact revenge from the blood of her enemies and bestow justice to those who share her creed."

When Knox looked again into Raven's eyes, he saw in the glistening pupils the reflection of his own devotion to her, and her unbreakable promise to live, and die, at his side. He pulled her close and kissed her hard and deeply. She groaned into his mouth and pressed her body against him, as ready to take and receive him that instant as she was when they joined in the cabin below their feet mere moments before.

Laughter and off-key singing reached them from the main deck. They parted and watched as Adelaide staggered between her two sailors, each holding tight to steady themselves and the others. They shouted rough oaths and butchered the melody of an obscene song while they climbed the stairs to the quarterdeck with great difficulty and many pauses to regain their balance.

Knox and Raven ran to the railing and watched, laughing, as the trio below made the summit and whooped loud cheers to celebrate their great triumph.

Knox pointed to Adelaide and shouted, "What happened to your habit, little nun?"

She lifted the bright skirt of many colors and swished it about as she swayed her hips, holding a bottle of rum in her other hand. "I cannot dance in that black cassock" she shouted, "and the time has come for me to *dance*!"

"Aye!" laughed Squid, spinning in unsteady circles. "Dance, an' many other happy uses of yer lovely body, eh, Addie?"

Raven laughed. "Addie?"

"Th' poorh nuh... nun" slurred Bilge, "known ahs Add, Add-duh-layd... fell overbohrd, I amh shorry to rephort. Addhie here ish a he-ealer, and shingher, and a dhanscher with noh ehqual."

Addie kissed the drunken sailor and pushed him hard, sending him rolling across the deck. "I think Queen Eve wove some magic into the very boards of this boat" she said, still shuffling back and forth in a happy two-step. "We all three feel younger by many years!"

Squid rushed her from behind and took her in a bear hug, grinding his hips against her bum and squeezing her ample breasts. She laughed like a girl, then lifted her heel in a mule kick to his crotch that sent him sprawling on the deck clutching his aching nutsack.

Knox and Raven burst into laughter. He hugged her from behind and whispered in her ear, "We have *Bonnie Bones*, we have the best mates, the best crew, and we have each other. Let's sail on and shake the world by its neck."

"Aye, aye, captain. Point the way. Onward to glory or death."

He turned her and kissed her again, tenderly this time. When they parted, he whispered against her lips, "To glory or death."

The monkey brothers watched from the crow's nest, Tim with a bemused smile, Tom with a lip-curled frown.

"Dear me" Tim said with a droll air, "how unspeakably maudlin they are. One would think they were reading lines from some love-struck schoolboy's copybook."

"People disgust me" Tom spat. "Just because they express a few glands and swap spit, they think they've seen the face of God."

"Perhaps they have. Or the nearest approximation, that transcendent spark that takes one out of oneself and into union with all life."

"Oh, fuck me, don't you start with that shit." Tom hiccupped and let out an acrid burp, his frown deepening to a grimace. "All that treacle from them plus a pedant's lecture from you ain't helping to settle my belly." He burped again. "Does this damn rocking never stop?"

"Never, I'm afraid."

"Oh well. Maybe 'll get used to it."

"It's certainly possible. Only a small percentage of people become permanently seasick."

"I ain't people, fuckstick!" The gurgling in the unhappy monkey's belly grew louder.

"Point taken. Well, when shall we reveal our status as stowaways? It would be prudent to stay out of sight for a time, but—"

Tom suddenly leaned over the crow's nest railing and retched, his agonized "Blaarrgh!" startling the three men and two women below. They looked up in time to see a watery mass of half-digested fruit cascade from the highest mast and splatter on the deck.

While Tom kept his head over the railing, gasping for air and spitting bile, Tim peered over the edge and saw every eye trained on their hideout.

"Well. I guess *that* ship has sailed."

END

SNEAK PEEK - The Madness of Stars

From Pirate Romance we travel to the far reaches of the universe for a rollicking sendup of the Space Opera genre – *The Madness of Stars*

Tales from the Quaquaverse is my ongoing series of original novellas aimed at spreading fun and laughter, thrills and chills, plus a bit of naughty pleasure thrown in just because. Each Tale is unique — a new world, all new characters, themes and genres — but they all celebrate the pleasure and privilege of being human, with all the dark and light shades that color our souls.

The "Quaquaverse" is merely my fanciful term for the source of every imaginable narrative — the metaverse of metaverses. The fountainhead of every fable, legend, myth and novel is like a blazing sun radiating stories in every direction - quaquaversally — the way a star in the cosmos radiates light. Each beam of light is a story, a world where a person lives who longs for love and adventure, a *Tale from the Quaquaverse.*

A.P. John

The Madness of Stars – Tales from the Quaquaverse 3

C hapter 1 – Royally Screwed

Ree'cult, earl of galactic segment Zed Alpha Nine, stood under the massive clear dome of the observation lounge at Groundport One watching the last of the royal yachts enter atmosphere in a blaze of fire, slow its descent and finally touch down on the landing field under heavy guard. He breathed a sigh of relief, confident that the three royal sons were now safe within the walls of the Imperial Palace on the ruling planet, Phallux. The bloodthirsty terrorists calling themselves the Free Universe Commando Korps would not assassinate a duke, one of their published goals, under Ree'cult's watch.

The distinguished elder in the long, shimmering foil robes of the noble classes ran a palm over his hairless, dark green scalp, wiping the perspiration that had formed while he nervously watched each of the three ducal boats land. There could be no trouble today, with the future of the galaxy hanging in the balance. The first step, ensuring the sons and their wives landed and were ensconced in the palace safely, was a success. Now Ree'cult was to bring them before their mother, Nygling — Nygling the Beautiful, the Terrible, the Carnal, the Insatiable, Empress of the Delta Mons galaxy and undisputed sovereign of the three-hundred-sixty thousand known planets. She had summoned her offspring to a secret meeting, the purpose of which she had not divulged even to her closest adviser, Ree'cult himself.

Commanding General Teh'nek entered the dome unnoticed by the earl. He walked soundlessly to his oldest friend and slapped him hard on the cheek in the traditional Phalluxian greeting.

"Ow! Teh'nek, you bastard son of a landless serf! How are you, my friend?"

"Much better now that the children are home and safe. Thanks to you."

"Just doing my job, General."

The officer, only a slightly lighter shade of green than his childhood friend, laughed quietly. "Save the modesty, Ree. These are dangerous times, and just doing our jobs may very well save the empire." He straightened his spine and tugged at the hem of his dark blue tunic, making the many medals pinned to his chest rattle and catch sparks of light.

"Perhaps. Did you run into any trouble?"

"No, thanks to your diplomatic skill. The Free Universe Commando Korps promised they would not interfere with the dukes' passages, and they kept their word."

Ree'cult scowled. "Hrmph. I arranged the terms, but I never trust those FUCKers any farther than I can throw the constellation Cat Butt."

"I share your distrust. I ordered regiments of SLITs to shadow the royal yachts from each end of their crackspace jumps."

"Secret Light Infantry Troopers? The terrorists did not spot them?"

"They posed as workers aboard old mining freighters. The ships were disguised attack boats, and if one of those FUCKers had so much as cracked into sight in a two-seater runabout, they'd have been C-beamed into oblivion."

A gleaming smile lit the earl's verdant face. "I say, good show old friend. Good show."

The general returned the smile. "Just doing my job, Your Excellency."

Ree'cult slapped the general on the cheek with a resounding smack and turned toward the exit. "Come with me, then, and help me do my next job."

"I suppose now you must extricate Her Majesty from her favorite pastime and remind her to attend to official affairs?

"Yes" the earl sighed, "not a pleasant task at any time, least of all now."

The two men stepped into a lift car. As the door closed, Ree'cult said, "Royal Orgy Room."

"What's the magic word?" asked the lift.

"Oh, blast it, these new-fangled machines. *Please?*"

The lift tisked and said, "You don't have to be snarky about it!" But the car began moving at high speed through the complex series of lift tunnels that connected every space in the Palace.

The general waited a moment before asking, "Have any idea what the Randy Royal is up to?"

Ree grinned but held a finger to his lips. "Careful with talk like that. Before the recent trouble, she was glad to take jokes in stride. But since the rebellion began claiming victories, she's ordered a clampdown on any talk that could be seen as seditious."

"I'll watch my tongue, then. So? Give me the gossip?"

The earl rubbed his hairless chin and frowned. "She's kept this under wraps, but from what I can glean, she means to abdicate."

"What?" The general's eyes widened, showing his iridescent gold irises and dilated pupils. "She can't be serious!"

"I can't tell with her anymore. She could be having us all on with the most elaborate practical joke. Or she could be deadly serious."

"But abdicate? After a thousand-cycle rule? She expanded the empire by twenty thousand planets, solidified our social order, and brought peace to the galaxy."

Ree shrugged. "That's all I know."

"Then one of the dukes would reign?"

"I suppose."

"But which?"

"I've never been able to tell who she favors. Less so now since she's been out of touch with all three for many cycles."

The general took a turn frowning. "If she means to abdicate, my friend, it does not bode well for the empire."

"Truly."

"The FUCKers grow bolder with every minor victory. You know they took over an entire continent on Intima Prime?"

"Yes. Dreadful."

"This is no time for weakness in the royal house."

"Agreed. But I am only her counselor, her First Advisor. I can do only so much."

The lift slowed and said, "Three-hundred, seventy-fifth floor. The Royal Orgy Room is first on the right."

The door slid open, and as the two men exited, they heard muffled but loud, thumping music and a dozen voices screaming in various stages of physical agony or ecstasy. A waft of bodily funk assaulted their nostrils.

The general sniffed and frowned. "I could find it with my eyes closed."

"Then why ask me?" said the bitchy lift as the door closed.

The music and screams grew louder as they approached the door. Ree'cult held his right hand over a sensor symbol and part of the wall vanished, inundating the men with a cacophony of raucous sounds and a wave of smells simultaneously arousing and disgusting. They walked through the portal and around a filmy screen to behold Empress Nygling in her glory.

Naked save for an anklet of precious jewels, her deep crimson skin glistening and dripping with sweat and the combined bodily fluids of some unknown number of her harem, Nygling stood bent over a luxurious bed taking a man's prodigious blue phallus as deeply into her throat as she could manage. Her long, silken white hair draped over one side of her beautiful face and tickled the man's balls as she rose and dove on his fat member. Behind her, a man from Intima Prime, skin so pale it was nearly translucent, was giving the Empress a hard fucking in both her orifices, equipped as he was with the double cock for which the males of his race were prized throughout the galaxy.

Two more Phalluxian Blues knelt beside the bed suckling her breasts, one male and one female, while a brace of others from several planets were strewn about, writhing like a litter of newborn pups, groaning, and screaming and laughing as they filled and painted each other with great jets of whatever their species ejaculated.

The Empress suddenly surrendered the blue cock, raised up and screamed "Now, you pale beast! Finish me! I can't wait!"

This spurred the man to fill his fist with her long locks and redouble his efforts. He slammed against the royal posterior with all his might, the wet slapping sounds of their bodies and his breathy grunts reverberating around the room. Her head stretched backward, Nygling rolled her eyes, dropped her jaw, and let out a long celebratory scream that inspired all the others to stop what they were doing, watch, smile, and applaud.

As the applause and her scream faded, she let her head fall back onto the blue man's belly and laughed like a woman both mad and in complete control of her faculties.

"Oh, fuck yes, that's how it's done boys! Did somebody record that? I want to show it to new recruits as a training aid."

The white man grinned and stepped back, pulling his double dick from her and watching as his spunk poured out in long, ropy strings, forming puddles on the shining stone floor. Nygling straightened, turned, and embraced the man with a deep tongue kiss and a squeeze to both of his now softening cocks.

The room sensed the royal finish, changed the music to lighter fare and lowered the volume. The rest of the sweaty entourage began filing out, laughing and kissing as they went.

Ree'cult tried a quiet clearing of his throat to get the Empress's attention, then another, to no effect. He finally said, "Begging your pardon, Your Highness?"

"Beg all you want" she said, speaking against her lover's mouth, "I won't listen unless you drop your robe and deliver just half of what this magnificent creature dealt me." She continued osculating the white man and grinding her hips against him in an obvious attempt to rouse him for an encore.

"But, Empress, Your Majesty, the dukes are here."

"What dukes?"

"Your... sons."

"What about 'em?"

"They're here."

"Why?"

"You summoned them."

The tall, svelte woman with impeccably clear and soft red royal skin stopped kissing the man, dropped her chin and said, "Shit."

The earl waited a moment before saying, "The dukes will gather in your war room within the hour, as you instructed, Your Majesty."

She kissed the man again, gave both his dicks a hard squeeze then smiled and slapped his muscular haunch. "Gotta go, lover. Matters of state and all that. But stay close and keep those things handy," she pointed down, "because I'll need a good hard ride when I'm done keeping the galaxy from falling apart."

The man grinned, kissed her hand and said, "Yes, Your Majesty."

"Now, get out or I can't think straight." She slapped his bottom again as he left.

Ree'cult said, "May I tell the royal sons when they can expect the Empress's presence?"

"Naw, let 'em sit and stew. I want a long, luxurious aromatherapy bath, a hot meal, and a smoke before I deal with that lot."

"As you wish, Majesty."

She eyed the general. "Hello Teh'nek. Shouldn't you be out rounding up terrorists and torturing them for intel?"

"I assure you, Majesty, I have many thousands performing that very task every moment of every day."

"Getting results?"

A man from Temptara gave up the location of a rebel broadcasting station, but his head came off before we could get entrance credentials for a secret raid."

"What did you do about it?"

"The Royal Navy Cruiser *Dogbone* flattened the facility and an area of some thousand dektares around it, just to be certain of a clean kill."

"Clean?"

Teh'nek hesitated. "There may have been some... collateral damage."

The Empress, regal and imposing despite, or perhaps because of, her nakedness, grinned. "Go carefully, general. I want every rebel and rebel sympathizer in the galaxy converted, imprisoned, or dead, down to their household pets. But if you leave behind too much *collateral damage*, the resentment among the people will snatch defeat from the jaws of victory."

"Yes, Your Majesty."

Nygling eyed Ree'cult, obviously anxious to execute his duties and wrangle her to the war room. "I see you peeing your pants over this meeting, Ree. Take a dose of Nebulax or something because I'll get there when I get there. You can tell the boys that and spike their drinks with Nebulax as well."

"Yes, Empress Nygling."

The ruler placed two fingers in her mouth, let out a piercing whistle and yelled, "Ballsack?"

A short, rotund, blue man in the red tunic and trousers of royal service, appeared from nowhere. "Yes, Your Majesty?"

"Round up a fresh squad, say, an even dozen. I don't care what the mix of races or sexes. Just tell 'em to stretch their jaw muscles and bring a towel."

"Yes, Empress."

She waved imperiously at the two men. "You two can stay and watch or go pound sand. Mama needs a tongue bath!"

TO BE CONTINUED...

Don't miss out!

Visit the website below and you can sign up to receive emails whenever A.P. John publishes a new book. There's no charge and no obligation.

https://books2read.com/r/B-A-IXVBB-ZAZLD

BOOKS 2 READ

Connecting independent readers to independent writers.

Also by A.P. John

Tales from the Quaquaverse
A Horse for My Kingdom
Sirens & Scoundrels

Watch for more at apjohn-author.com.